THE DEADLY DOG-BONE CAPER

THE DEADLY DOG-BONE CAPER

•

Book Three
in
The Jennifer Gray Veterinarian Mystery Series

•

GEORGETTE LIVINGSTON

AVALON BOOKS
THOMAS BOUREGY AND COMPANY, INC.
401 LAFAYETTE STREET
NEW YORK, NEW YORK 10003

© Copyright 1996 by Georgette Livingston
Library of Congress Catalog Card Number: 95-95221
ISBN 0-8034-9158-1

420792 c1

PRINTED IN THE UNITED STATES OF AMERICA
ON ACID-FREE PAPER
BY HADDON CRAFTSMEN, SCRANTON, PENNSYLVANIA

For Sally Allen, who always loved a good mystery.

Chapter One

Jennifer Gray lifted her face to the soft breeze and the fiery ball of orange as it rose in the east. Clouds, like crimson ribbons of gossamer, drifted across the horizon, and above, the early morning sky had turned carnation pink. She had lived in Calico, Nebraska, all her life, and yet she still had a difficult time trying to describe a late August sunrise. Her grandfather probably said it best: angels had kissed the sky with their paintbrushes, putting the summer season to rest. And this morning it seemed even more spectacular because of the inner peace and contentment she felt. They had just saved a dog's life by performing emergency surgery.

The call from the frantic owner had been

patched through to Ben Copeland's home around four A.M., and he in turn had called her. It was a "red alert." The dog had a bone blocking its windpipe, and if they didn't act fast, they would lose him. It wasn't the first time Ben had called her at odd hours, and it wouldn't be the last. Ben was grooming her to take over for him when he retired, and although she was an accredited D.V.M., this was her first job after graduating from veterinary school at Michigan State University, and she needed all the experience she could get before Ben could comfortably walk away from the practice that had taken him years to build. More importantly, she had to prove to the town that she was no longer "little Jennifer Gray," the pastor's tomboy granddaughter. She was now Jennifer Gray, D.V.M., the pastor's "grown-up" granddaughter, who was more than qualified to care for all manner of animals and pets, large and small.

Now, with the dog—an Airedale terrier with a touch of standard poodle—resting comfortably, and the anxious owner on his way home, Jennifer was taking a well-deserved coffee break out in the small garden area behind the clinic, watching "the angels paint the sky" as the sweet scent of rich earth and flowers wafted through the air around her. She smiled, thinking about Ben's wife, Irene, and how insistent she had been when she put in the garden, claiming they had to have *someplace* to take their breaks that would get them out of the clinic and away from "all those antiseptic smells." She'd even added two wrought-iron chairs and a small table, and had tacked up a bird feeder to a nearby elm tree.

Ben said the whole thing was frivolous, but that hadn't stopped him from enjoying their little retreat whenever he could. At the moment, he was making his way across the graveled parking area, carrying a cup of coffee in one hand and a folder in the other.

Ben was a tall man in his early sixties, with a weathered face, a mop of gray, unruly hair, and warm hazel eyes. He had an ulcer and was on a special diet, but he refused to give up coffee or orange soda.

Ben sat down, placed the cup and folder on the table, and gave Jennifer a lopsided grin. "You were the one who figured out the bone was further down, that we weren't going to be able to get it out with forceps, and suggested going in by way of a tracheotomy, Jennifer, so I thought you might like to fill out the report, and sign your name."

It was Ben's way of making her feel like she

was a part of the clinic, and she loved him for it. "I'd be glad to," Jennifer said, lifting her blond hair off her neck in a casual stretch. "I suppose we should have given Mr. Wise a lecture on the kinds of bones he can give his dog, but he was so upset, I didn't have the heart to jump on him."

They were both wearing pale blue lab coats over their clothing, and Ben unbuttoned his and adjusted the collar. "I know, but he isn't going to get off that easily. I plan to talk to him when he comes in to pick up the dog. Looked like a chicken bone to me. And that's the worst kind."

Jennifer was studying the file, and read from the "new patient" form. "The dog's name is Einstein, Mr. Wise's first name is Dan, and he's been in town three months. Oh, oh. He works at the dairy, and lives in one of the company cottages."

Ben snorted. "Fancy name for shacks. But with an owner like Elmer Dodd, what can you expect?"

Jennifer shuddered, thinking about Elmer Dodd. The man was a blight on the town. A true nemesis, who thought of no one but himself, and the profits and gains he could acquire using sneaky, unethical tactics. His loathsome behavior went back years, and included things like trying to sell outdated milk, mistreatment of his cows, evicting a family of seven from one of his rental houses because they were a month behind on the rent, and cutting down the largest and most beautiful American elm tree in all of Peace County, simply because it obstructed the view from his living-room window. Though nothing could quite compare with his latest scheme.

Because he was planning to run for mayor next year and needed a praiseworthy image, Elmer Dodd had generously donated a plot of land for the senior citizens' center, and all the building materials they would need. And because the senior citizens wanted to do most of the work themselves, he had even hired a construction crew out of North Platte to oversee the operation. All quite admirable but for a couple of things most people had overlooked, or had decided to ignore, because Elmer Dodd also had power and money, and knew how to play that to his advantage: the plot of arid land south of town was next to the waste disposal site; there wasn't a tree or bush on the property; the working conditions were deplorable; and the building supplies substandard.

Jennifer had been home only a few weeks after graduating from veterinary school when she found out about it, and was so appalled she could hardly stand it. What was the town thinking of? Why had they let it happen, when they could have easily donated any one of the numerous parks in Calico for the project? Most of the senior citizens were descendants of the people who had founded the town, and deserved much more than a view of a garbage dump! Even worse was the way they had blindly accepted the plot of land, as though Elmer Dodd was doing them a big favor, thus almost assuring disaster.

Jennifer was about to take her complaints to the mayor and the planning commission, when a swift and turbulent summer storm had swept through Calico, bringing down the roof of the nearly completed structure, and leaving behind a plot of land full of sinkholes, which meant the building would have eventually collapsed anyway. There had been some injuries and, finally, the senior citizens had come to their senses. They'd formed a coalition, hired attorney Willy Ashton, and had sued Elmer Dodd. Jennifer and Willy shared a warm, comfortable relationship that had originated in their childhood, and as far as she was concerned, they couldn't have retained a more qualified attorney to represent them. Unfortunately, Elmer Dodd had been thinking ahead, and had come up with a way to turn it all around in his favor. He had openly apologized, feigned innocence—he had no idea the property would be worthless as a building site—and settled out of court for an undisclosed amount of money, after which the town couldn't do much more than praise him for his generosity. But there had been an upside. The town had finally rallied to the cause, and had donated White River Park for the project, thus leaving a good deal of money in the senor citizens' coffer, and Elmer Dodd with the arid plot of land. Though there was talk now that the town might buy the land from him so the waste disposal site could be expanded.

Ben waved a hand in front of Jennifer's face. "You look a million miles away, Jennifer."

"I was just thinking about Elmer Dodd. He's such a despicable man. And there he is, living in a mansion while he builds shacks for his employees. You have to wonder why they put up with it. Why don't they move someplace else?"

"I've heard the rent is reasonable, Jennifer, and with the economy the way it is today, just about everybody is trying to save a buck."

"The shacks should be rent free, considering what Dodd pays his employees."

Ben lifted a brow. "And how do you know what Dodd pays the hired help?"

"Says right here under the listing for credit information. Dan Wise makes minimum wage. Makes me wonder how he's going to pay for Einstein's emergency surgery.''

Ben shook his head. ''Money has never been an issue with me.''

''I know, and that's why you can't afford to update the equipment, or refurbish the clinic. I would never turn away somebody who couldn't pay either, Ben, but the town is growing, and the clinic should be growing too. Regardless of what Grandfather says about the town's growing pains, we have to accept it and move on.''

''And I suppose you have another dream?''

''As a matter of fact, I do. Looking ahead to the future, I can see a full-scale animal hospital. We certainly have the room to expand.''

Ben grunted. ''With a staff of twenty?''

''If that's what it takes. Right now, we're a staff of three, because our facilities are limited. In a couple of years, Tina will be going off to college and then veterinary school, you'll be retired, and I'll be alone.''

''Unless you can find another gem like Tina Allen. We hired her to help out around the clinic, do all the menial tasks, and look at her now.''

''Yes, look at her now! She gives us one hundred percent because she has a dream, Ben. I had a dream, too, and I've fulfilled it by coming home as a full-fledged vet. But it doesn't stop there, and it won't for Tina, either. Not many years ago, a vet was known as little more than a horse doctor. Today, he or she has to be a little bit of everything, including physician, surgeon, psychologist, pathologist, and everything in between. The United States is in the middle of a remarkable revolution in veterinary medicine and, because of it, most animal hospitals compare with human hospitals, with state-of-the-art equipment, like electrocardiograph machines, and the latest in laboratory diagnostic equipment, and . . .'' Jennifer's voice trailed off. ''I'm sorry. I didn't mean to get carried away.''

Ben patted her hand. ''It's okay, and I understand. But I'll admit it makes me a little sad. You youngsters will be carrying on in the modern world of animal science, while I'm sitting on my porch in a rocking chair, wishing I was thirty years younger.''

Jennifer felt a fullness around her heart. ''You won't be ready for a rocking chair for a long, long time, Ben, and besides, nobody, not even us youngsters, can replace what you've given our profession. Years and years of dedication and love, and the experience that comes with it. It's because of people like you that we are where we are today. And don't you ever forget it.''

There was a shimmer of tears in Ben's eyes when he said, ''You're the real gem, Jennifer, and don't *you* ever forget it. Now, why don't you write up the report, and go home and get some breakfast. Maybe take the rest of the morning off.''

''Tina isn't coming in, Ben. Remember, you gave her the week off?''

''No big deal. It's going to be a slow morning.''

She eyed him intently. ''You haven't said, but why did you give her the week off?''

She's only sixteen, and needs a little time to be a kid before school starts. She's going camping with her folks.''

''My, my. How you've changed. As I recall, you had a fit when Bobby Kanter and Kyle Wallace quit early in the summer, because they said it was interfering with their fun.''

''Yeah, well, those two were different. They were working here because it was a job, not because they wanted to become veterinarians. Tina does more work than they ever did. More than the two of 'em put together.''

Jennifer grinned. ''Well, now that you've got that off your chest, I have a suggestion. Why don't *you* go home and get some breakfast. I'm sure

Irene would be delighted. I'll bet if you gave her a big kiss, she might even let you put a sprinkle of cinnamon on your oatmeal."

Ben made a face. "To tell you the truth, I've been on this blamed diet for so long, it's beginning to become a habit."

"Uh-huh, and your ulcer is getting better, even with all the coffee and orange sodas you drink, so that has to count for something. Give Irene my love, and take your time. I can handle things here."

After Ben left, although Jennifer felt the warm glow that came from love and friendship, she felt overwhelming sadness, too, thinking about the day when Ben would finally retire, and how much she was going to miss him.

Jennifer finished the report, looked in on Einstein, and then spent the next hour cleaning up the operating room. The bone that had been removed from Einstein's trachea was in a metal pan. She started to throw it out, but then reconsidered. She would save it, and show it to Dan Wise, after Ben gave him a lecture.

She had a Baggie in one hand, and the bone in the other, when she felt an unexpected chill. It really was a strange bone, and didn't look like a chicken bone at all. It looked more like a . . . Jennifer blinked to clear her vision, and took the bone over to the window for more light. Suddenly the word "phalanges" came to mind, meaning digits or toes in an animal or human, but could mean digits or *fingers* in a human. She shook her head, put the bone in the plastic bag, but couldn't shake the apprehension she felt. Although there were many similarities in the skeletal makeup of all vertebrates, differences had evolved over many centuries. She looked down at her own fingers, mentally considered their skeletal structure, and sucked in her breath. She didn't see how it could be possible, but she knew in her heart the bone they had removed from Einstein's trachea had been part of a human finger.

Jennifer dialed Ben's home phone number, and tried to keep her voice under control when she said, "Have you eaten?"

"Yeah, a bowl of oatmeal. What is it, Jennifer, you sound 'funny.' "

"I think you'd better come back to the clinic."

"The dog . . ."

"No, Einstein is okay. I don't want to discuss it over the phone."

Ben groaned, muttered he was on his way, and hung up.

While Jennifer waited, she swallowed two aspirin with a large glass of water, and considered the possibilities. If what she suspected was true, that meant that somewhere in or around the town of Calico, Einstein had found the skeletal remains of a human body. Little wonder she was getting a headache!

Ten minutes later, Ben found Jennifer in his office, looking pale and fidgety. She handed him the Baggie and said, "It's a human bone, Ben. And my guess, it's one of the phalanges from a finger."

Ben ran a hand through his gray hair. "Good Lord, Jennifer . . ."

"Look at it, Ben. Really look at it. I know at first glance it could be taken for the thighbone of a chicken, or some other form of poultry, but the shape is wrong, and it's too wide."

Ben sat down at his cluttered desk and stared at the bone, trying to see what Jennifer was seeing. Finally, he looked up at her and sighed. "You know, I should tell you you're nuts, that it isn't possible. I should remind you that you're the young lady who has always had an overactive imagination, but a part of me is reminding myself that you're also the young lady who, in a matter of a few short months, helped the sheriff put a fugitive behind bars and find a couple of missing boys. And none of that was luck. You might have a vivid imagination, but you also have an intuitiveness that nobody can deny, or should. And that's the only reason I'm going to take the bone to the hospital lab, though I don't think I have to tell you what might happen if you're right."

Jennifer shivered. "No, you don't. I can take the bone to the hospital. . . ."

"I think it might be better if I take it, Jennifer. Let's try and keep you out of this, for as long as possible. You've already got the whole town's attention. Good Lord in heaven, what next?"

Jennifer gave Ben a wan smile, but her thoughts were galloping ahead. She also remembered what one of her friends in veterinary school had said to her the day before graduation. "I can't imagine why you would want to go into practice in a small, sleepy little town. Calico, Nebraska? I'll bet it isn't even on the map. You're going to be bored to death, Jennifer. Betcha within six months you'll be heading for the bright lights of a big city, where things *really* happen." Jennifer sighed. If her friend only knew. *Everything* seemed to happen in Calico.

After Ben had gone, Jennifer checked on Einstein, and tried to keep busy, dusting furniture that had already been dusted, and mopping the floor that didn't need mopping. The first step would be to find out where the dog had gotten the bone, and it wasn't going to be easy.

Jennifer was making a pot of coffee when Ben walked in two hours later. And she didn't even have to look at him. She could hear it in his steps. Still, she braced herself for his words.

"Sorry I took so long," he said wearily, "but I wanted to wait for the results. You were right. The bone is part of a human finger. I took it to Sheriff Cody, and he wants to see you as soon as possible. Guess that shouldn't be a surprise. The two of you are getting to be pretty good friends. I'm surprised he isn't trying to talk you into becoming one of his deputies."

His stab at humor brought a smile to her face in spite of the way she felt. *Thinking* it was a human finger was one thing, but it was quite another to find out it was true.

Jim Cody had been the sheriff of Peace County for as long as Jennifer could remember. He was a large, husky, gray-haired man with a warm smile, and had been elected to his position over and over again because he was the best of the best. At the present time the sheriff's department—nestled between City Hall and the library, and a block from the courthouse—had eight deputies, four patrol cars, not counting the sheriff's, and Nettie Balkin, who was the secretary, clerk and dispatcher, and kept everybody on their toes. She was plump and had a warm smile, too, but she was tough, though she didn't look so tough this morning, as Jennifer made her way into the office. She was absently pulling at her gray hair, snapping gum, and pacing the floor.

The sheriff looked upset too, but he managed a smile and said, "The coffee is good and strong. Help yourself."

"Good thing it's strong," Nettie grumbled, pointing at the bone on the sheriff's desk.

The sheriff was looking at it, too. "I've got the report from the hospital here, but maybe you can fill me in. Ben gave me a few particulars, like how you took the bone out of a dog's windpipe early this morning, but other than that, he seemed to be in a hurry. Looked uncomfortable."

Nettie snapped, "I can understand that. He's probably wondering what this town is coming to. What happened to the good old days when all we had to do was worry about speeding tickets, parking tickets, the crazy Wilson brothers and their Saturday night brawls, or maybe an occasional altercation out at Boodie's Roadhouse? Now we've got fugitives, kidnappers, and dead bodies.''

''Well, we don't really have any dead bodies *yet*, '' Jennifer reminded Nettie. ''Only a part of a finger.''

''I know, but the way things have been happening around here, I'm starting to feel real nervous. I wake up every morning and ask myself, what next? Is this going to be a sane day, or a crazy day?''

The sheriff sighed. ''Ben said you haven't talked to the dog's owner about this, Jennifer, but I don't suppose he'll . . .'' He looked down at his notes. ''Okay, the man's name is Wise. Don't suppose Mr. Wise will be much help. Dogs can dig up the darndest things. Hmmm. The dog's name is Einstein. That ought to tell us something!''

''Well, we still have to talk to him, Sheriff. Did Ben tell you where Mr. Wise lives?''

''No, he didn't.''

''He works for Elmer Dodd at the dairy, and lives in one of the company cottages.''

Sheriff Cody rolled his eyes. ''Terrific. Just what we need, another run-in with Dodd.''

''Maybe he doesn't have to know. At least not yet. Maybe nobody has to know until after we've done a little investigating, and know what we're dealing with.''

The sheriff shook his head. ''*We*?''

''Well, that's why you wanted to talk to me, isn't it? You want my help?''

Nettie finally managed a grin. ''She knows you better than you know yourself, Sheriff. Admit you look forward to seeing her smiling face, and listening to all those pearls of wisdom she has stored away in her beautiful head.''

The sheriff poked at the plastic bag with his finger. ''What about Ben? Every time I take you away from him, I feel guilty. You're a vet, Jennifer. You're in training to take over when Ben retires. And that's what you should be doing, vet stuff. Cop stuff is for cops.''

''I do plenty of 'vet stuff,' Sheriff, and Ben doesn't plan on retiring yet. Besides, he understands. He said just this morning he's surprised you haven't tried to talk me into becoming a deputy.''

The sheriff sighed. ''I would if I thought that's what you wanted. You'd make a good cop. But then you're a bang-up vet, too.''

Jennifer batted her eyelashes at him. ''It's called multitalented,'' she teased.

''Uh-huh, and you'd probably make a good

psychologist. After all, you're the one who got Cracker Martin back into the land of the living, instead of hibernating out on his pig farm, and you've even gotten us to shake hands now and again, though I have to admit he can still rile me up. Just the other day, he mentioned Addy. Said he considered all that time she was dating me before she married him wasted. I tried to tell him I wasn't dating her then, that she was just coming to me for sympathy because he was such a jerk, but he wouldn't listen. Felt like busting the old goat in the nose, but then I thought about you, and decided facing your disapproval wasn't worth it.'' A slight grin tugged at the corners of his mouth. ''That's just a fancy way of saying, if I punched Cracker out, I'd have to answer to you.''

At the mention of Cracker's name, Jennifer felt a special warmth, and sadness. His beautiful Saint Bernard, Elvis, had literally given his life to save the Peterson boys, who had gotten trapped in a cave-in up in the hills. Elvis was buried on Cracker's farm, under a spreading peachleaf willow, and the plaque, awarded to Elvis for his heroism by the town, rested on the mantel in his living room, beside Addy's picture. Now all he had were memories.

Jennifer felt her throat constrict, but managed

to say, "It isn't a pig farm, Sheriff, even though Cracker raises pigs, and it's silly to carry a grudge for years and years. Life is too short, too precious."

The sheriff nodded. "And if I forget that, you're gonna remind me. Okay, so how do you want to handle this?"

"How do *I* want to handle it?" Jennifer asked incredulously.

"Yeah, you. Like Nettie said, you're the one who always comes up with the good ideas. I figure you've already decided where there is one bone, there could be more."

Pleased by the compliment, but feeling a little guilty, too, because the man looked so weary, and was probably wondering where all this was going to lead, Jennifer said, "I think we should keep a low profile, until we get some answers. I'll go back to the clinic and call Mr. Wise. I'll tell him we have to talk to him about his dog. That shouldn't raise any suspicions. I'd question him over the phone, but I much prefer to do it face to face. That way, I can look in his eyes, and know if he's telling the truth. Anyway, when he gets to the clinic, I'll question him, in a roundabout way, of course, and then I'll call you. You can decide how you want to handle it from there."

"Sounds good to me, but I can't wait around for your call. Have some cattle rustling going on near the county line, and I'll be heading out in a few minutes."

"Okay, then we can connect later."

The sheriff nodded, but Jennifer could see the look in his eyes. He didn't like the idea of finding a human skeleton any more than she did, and he had his fingers and toes crossed there would be some other reasonable explanation.

They had just finished lunch when Dan Wise arrived at the clinic. Ben shook the man's hand, and cleared his throat. "I'll let my assistant explain this to you, because she is directly responsible for saving your dog's life."

Dan Wise sighed with relief. "Then he's okay? When you called, I thought . . ."

He was a large man, possibly in his forties, with a head of sandy-colored hair and clear brown eyes. He was wearing jeans and a brown shirt the color of his eyes, and it was obvious he cared a great deal for his dog.

Jennifer replied, "Einstein is fine, Mr. Wise, but next time he might not be so lucky, and that's why we wanted to talk to you. I know you're on your lunch hour, so we'll get right to the point."

He shrugged. "No hurry. Not much going on today anyway. The boss is in Omaha, and things sort of stop when he isn't around. Well, they don't exactly stop, but at least we get to relax a little, and don't have to keep looking over our shoulders."

"I take it your boss is a taskmaster?"

"Worse than that."

"What do you do at the dairy, Mr. Wise?"

"I help clean the milking machines morning and night. In between, I do odd jobs."

"And you live in one of the company cottages?"

He grimaced, and nodded. "It isn't much. Just a couple of drafty rooms out near the barns. I wanted to rent the two-bedroom cottage near the office, but the boss uses it for storage."

"Do you have a wife?"

"No wife. Not anymore. It's just me and Einstein."

"I can tell you care about your dog, Mr. Wise, and that's all the more reason for you to understand how important this is. As we explained to you after the surgery, Einstein had a bone stuck in his trachea, or windpipe. If it had gone further down into the esophagus, we would have had to open up his chest."

Ben spoke up. "Chicken and fish bones, or any small bone, can be mighty bad for a dog. If you have to give him a bone, make it a *big* beef bone. Actually, commercial milk bones are just as good. Good for the teeth, too. If you're thinking about the expense, you might want to weigh the price of a few boxes of milk bones against your vet bill."

The man's mouth turned down. "About the vet bill . . ."

"Let's not worry about that right now," Jennifer said. "It's more important for you to understand . . ."

"I didn't give Einstein the bone," Dan Wise said. "He got it somewhere else. He has a habit of wandering. Very curious . . . *smart*. That's why I named him Einstein. Even as a puppy, he'd take off for hours at a time."

"Okay, then maybe we'd better try and reconstruct where Einstein might have gone last night. If he found one bone, he could find another. And that's something else. It isn't a good idea to let a pet wander like that. His world is full of 'doggie disasters.' I realize you don't have a fenced-in yard, but if you could keep him in the house . . ."

"Lord, I couldn't do that. Try and keep him in and I'd be a raving lunatic. He scratches at the door and howls. Mr. Dodd said I could keep him with me, as long as he behaves. But if I get any complaints . . .''

Jennifer sighed. ''So when Einstein decides to roam, do you know where he goes?''

''I've never followed him, if that's what you mean.''

''Do you have any ideas?''

''Haven't a clue.''

''What about the condition of his coat, after he returns home—is it dirty or full of burrs?''

''No, but sometimes he comes home muddy.''

''And last night?''

''Didn't notice.''

''Do you know how long he was gone last night?''

''Probably two hours. I was listening to the radio when he came back, and he was breathing funny. Didn't think too much about it until later. I went to bed, and he woke me up gasping. That's when I realized he wasn't getting enough air, and I knew I had to get help. Guess it was near four when I finally called. To tell you the truth, I didn't know what to do. I mean I saw the number for the clinic listed in the phone book, and it said 'call day or night,' but I didn't think that meant in the *middle* of the night.''

"If we're not here," Jennifer said, "the switch-board transfers the emergency calls to Dr. Copeland's house. Day or night."

"Guess I should've called sooner . . ."

Jennifer gave him a reassuring smile. "What's done is done, Mr. Wise, and fortunately Einstein is going to make a full recovery. You'll be able to take him home as soon as we remove the tube from his throat."

"When will that be?"

"Probably the day after tomorrow. You'll also have to keep him in the house until the incision has healed, but perhaps if you explain what happened to Elmer Dodd . . ."

He chuckled without humor. "Apparently you don't know Elmer Dodd."

"I know him," Jennifer said. "Everybody knows him. Tell you what, if he gives you any problems, send him to me."

Jennifer heard Ben's intake of breath, and pressed on. "We don't want you to worry, Mr. Wise. We'll take good care of Einstein, and we'll call you when he's ready to be released."

"And now we don't know a cotton-picking thing more than we did before," Ben said, after the man had gone.

"Sure we do. Dan Wise loves his dog, and I

have the feeling he'll do whatever he can to change Einstein's wandering habits. And we know he isn't the killer. Everything he said was the truth.

"Killer? Are you saying you think somebody murdered somebody, and then buried the body?"

"Don't you?"

Ben sighed. "I was kinda hoping there would be another explanation. Like maybe the storm unearthed a coffin at the cemetery."

"And Einstein discovered a way to open the lid? Hardly, and you know how old Bert Levy takes care of things at the cemetery. If the storm had uncovered a coffin, he would have discovered it the next morning, and would have gotten the whole town into an uproar."

"So now what?" Ben said dejectedly.

"We wait until Einstein has recovered from the surgery, and hope he'll lead us to the spot where he found the bone. And I'm not talking about letting him roam. I'm talking about walking him with a leash."

"That could be at least a couple of weeks, Jennifer. . . ."

"I know, but if the bone was attached to a skeleton, the skeleton isn't going anywhere. Meanwhile, we have a clinic to run. Let's concentrate on that.''

''Yeah, right,'' Ben grumbled, tossing his lunch bag in the trash. ''I know you too well, Jennifer. There is a mystery to solve, and you're going to do your darndest to solve it. What more can I say?''

Jennifer gave him an innocent grin. ''That you know I have no intentions of waiting a couple of weeks. What more can *I* say?''

Chapter Two

"Well, my goodness! Is it really little Jennifer Gray? My, my, how you've changed. Of course, I haven't seen you in years, and everybody has 'ta get older. Still blond, I see, and the same big blue eyes. I heard you were home for good now, and working for old Ben Copeland at the animal hospital. I don't have any animals, so I never get out 'ta that end of town, except when I go 'ta the cemetery and visit my mother, God rest her soul. Not that I don't like animals. Don't get around much anymore, so guess it's a good thing I don't have a pet. Lots of work. Too much work, and expensive, too. A can of dog food costs more than a can of soup. Or maybe that's the other way around. I heard you are still up 'ta your old ways, always looking for trouble, and finding it. I've been reading about all your 'ventures in the newspaper. You've become quite a celebrity. Only been home from that fancy school in Michigan a little while, too. My, my, you always had energy 'ta burn. Doing this and doing that. Always doing something for one cause or another. My mother, God rest her soul, used 'ta call you 'that mischievous little Gray girl.' Of course, back then it was easy 'ta keep track of your shenanigans, without having 'ta read about you in the newspaper. The population was about five hundred then. Now I'll bet it's close 'ta two thousand, or maybe that's twenty thousand. No, guess it's about five. I have a hard time remembering things these days, but that's what happens when you get older. Too bad things can't stay the same. Too many people now, and that big old mall out on Route five. I heard it's got ten stores. Even a J. C. Penney. Of course they've got a lot of building going on out there, too. Apartments and even a mobile home park. Or is it a trailer park? Guess you're still living with your grandpa and Emma? Haven't seen them in ages, either. Used 'ta go to church all the time but, like I said, I don't get around much anymore. Hmmm. Emma Morrison must be in her sixties now. Is she still overweight?''

When the woman stopped to take a breath, Jennifer said, "It's good to see you too, Miss Anderson. Actually, Grandfather and Emma have both lost a lot of weight. I brought home some exercise equipment from Michigan, and taught them how to use it, and Grandfather jogs to the river every morning."

"Hmmm, lot of good that will do the way Emma cooks. All that fattening food. I remember one time we had a potluck after church, and she fixed meat, potatoes and gravy, or maybe it was turkey and gravy. Anyway, she baked a huge chocolate cake. I learned to cook wholesome food when my mother, God rest her soul, was alive. She had a good appetite, even when the end was upon her."

"Emma's cooking has changed, too, Miss Anderson. She understands the importance of cooking healthy food. I bought her several cookbooks full of fat-free, low-calorie recipes, and she uses the recipes all the time."

"Hmmm. Does Emma's hair still look like a Brillo pad? Always looked like a Brillo pad looks after scrubbing a sink full of pots and pans. Let's see. She's been your grandpa's housekeeper for years. Long before you went 'ta live with them. And that grandpa of yours! Such a handsome man. You know I went 'ta school with him. Wesley

Gray. We called him Wes. Always knew he'd end up looking like Santa Claus when he got older. White hair, fat pink cheeks, and plump around the middle. Hmmm. You say he's thinned down? Hmmm.'' She squinted her eyes. ''You look like your mama. She was such a pretty little thing, with all that golden hair. Oh, and that daddy of yours was so handsome. I remember going 'ta the pharmacy even when I didn't need a thing, just so I could look at his handsome face. Oh, and he always looked so professional in that white pharmacy jacket, and he was always so intent, filling prescriptions. Never cheated anybody, either.'' She lowered her voice. ''Got 'ta watch the old coot who runs the pharmacy now. I count every pill he gives me. Have 'ta count my change, too. Never had 'ta do that when your daddy was alive. It was such a tragedy when your mama and daddy were killed in that awful boating accident. Or was it an auto accident? I remember, it was an auto accident. Well, listen 'ta me, dredging up old memories.''

Jennifer had stopped by the market to pick up a few things on her way home, and had been so intent on what she was doing, she hadn't seen Cottie Anderson until the woman had cornered her in the produce department, between the carrots and the lettuce. And now she was stuck, because there was no way to get away from Cottie gracefully. Nor had the woman aged gracefully. She was still tall, square, and built like a tank, but now had a bezillion wrinkles. And she still wore her horned-rimmed glasses down on her nose, which gave her a haughty look. She was dying her hair bright red these days, and had applied round circles of rouge to her cheeks to match. A red and white polka-dot flouncy dress, little white gloves, and white sneakers completed the outrageous picture.

Cottie looked at the wedge of watermelon in Jennifer's shopping cart and frowned. "Don't tell me your grandpa has given up growing vegetables. I can remember going 'ta his little house after church and picking red tomatoes right off the vine. I remember one time I took home baskets of strawberries, too. He always grew too much."

Jennifer managed a smile. "Grandfather still grows vegetables, Miss Anderson, and the best strawberries in Calico, but the space is too limited to grow watermelons, what with Emma's beautiful flower garden. . . ."

"She still grows flowers, huh? I can't work in the garden anymore. I have a bad hip. Bad knee, too. Suppose I should go over 'ta the new hospital across the river and let them look at all my ailments, but then I'd feel guilty for leaving old Doc

Chambers. Thing is, he's almost eighty, and his eyesight isn't too good. Should retire, that's what he should do. Then I could go to the hospital and I wouldn't feel guilty.''

Jennifer nodded at the carton of milk in Cottie's basket. ''I see you're buying milk at the store instead of from the dairy.''

Cottie snapped, ''I wouldn't buy milk from Elmer Dodd if he had the last holstein cow in the county. Oh, I know he ships his milk 'ta that big outfit in North Platte, and it comes right back here 'ta us, all packaged up, but at least I know *they* know what they're doing, and that what I buy in the store is fresh, and pasteurized.'' She lowered her voice again. ''I heard Elmer is running for mayor next year. Boy, isn't that something! He'd better be thankful we've got so many new people in town. People who don't know about his shifty ways. Was the smartest thing Bernice ever did, leaving that man. 'Course she left with a traveling salesman, so don't suppose her life has been any better since.'' Cottie sniffed. ''You know, that was a real surprise, 'cause I always thought she was sweet on Joe Daily.''

''That name isn't familiar.''

''Worked at the dairy. Tall, strapping, handsome man. Worked there about a year, and then he was gone like a leaf on the breeze. Bernice left like a leaf on the breeze, too. But like I said, was the smartest thing she ever did. 'Course I had 'ta start using Martha Brown for a hairdresser after that. And she never could compare with Bernice. Bernice used 'ta make the prettiest little curls on top of my head, and always got the color just right. Think I was blond, back in those days, or maybe I was a brunet. Can't remember things like I used 'ta, but then I'm getting older.''

''I didn't know Elmer Dodd's wife that well, Miss Anderson. I was around twelve when all that happened. And it was never the topic of conversation around our house.''

''Well, I can understand that, what with your grandpa being the pastor of the Calico Christian Church and all, but lots of folks in town talked, and they all had something 'ta say. Nobody was surprised when Elmer didn't get married again. Who would want him? And most folks felt it was God's way that he never had any kids. He built that big old house north of the river for Bernice, and now he rattles around in it, getting older, and crankier and meaner. I know he's only in his twenties . . . No, that's wrong. Has 'ta be somewhere in his mid- 'ta late forties, but he looks a lot older. That's what happens when a body frowns all the time. Oh, but he wasn't frowning the other day when I saw him in the Post Office, or maybe it was the Mercantile. No siree. He was all smiles, sucking in his fat stomach and puffing out his chest 'cause he gave the senior citizens a bunch of money. I had 'ta bite my tongue. The only reason he gave them all that money was 'ta keep them from suing him. Read about that in the newspaper, too. I also heard about the land he gave them 'ta build the senior citizens' center. Right next 'ta the dumps. Can you beat that? I about had a heart attack. They were crazy 'ta take it. Well at least the town came 'ta its senses and gave the old folks the White River Park. Lots of trees and flowers. Lots of room. I just might join up after they get the place built. Of course, I don't get around much anymore. Hard for me 'ta drive.''

Cottie Anderson chattered on for a good ten minutes longer before Jennifer could finally make her escape, and by then, she was exhausted, and had the beginning of another headache.

The little white clapboard house tucked in beside the church was a welcome sight as Jennifer made her way along the flagstone path, bordered on one side by Emma's colorful flowers, and on the other by her grandfather's vegetables. Both gardens looked a little shabby now, because summer was drawing to a close. It wouldn't be long before the ground was covered with snow. And with that thought came another. It was imperative they find the rest of the skeleton before the first winter storm.

"Oh, oh, bad day, huh?" Wes said, as Jennifer climbed the steps to the porch.

She put the grocery bag down on the side table, where Emma had set out a pitcher of iced tea and glasses, and breathed in the sweet scent of honeysuckle that grew in profusion over one end of the porch. "It was an eventful day, Grandfather," she said, kissing his cheek before sitting down in the white wicker chair beside him. "And then I ran into Cottie Anderson . . ."

Emma stepped out on the porch, let the screen door slam, and snorted, "I haven't talked to that crazy old warhorse in years. I see her now and again, but you'd better believe I head the other way. Never could stand all her busybody gossip and nonstop chatter which, for the most part, never made a lick of sense. Just like her mother. Crazy as a bedbug. Best thing that ever happened was when she quit coming to church."

Wes shook his head. "There will always be a place in my church for Cottie Anderson, Emma."

"Hrump! If God intended her to be there, God would see to it she got there."

Emma was poking her nose in the grocery bag, and Jennifer said, "I picked up a wedge of watermelon, a carton of cottage cheese, Saltine crackers, and a few bananas."

Emma's brows furrowed together over dark blue eyes. "And I suppose that's going to be your dinner?"

"Depends on what you're cooking," Jennifer teased.

"Broiled ground round patties, baked potatoes and steamed zucchini, Miss Smarty Pants. Help yourself to the iced tea. I squeezed in some lemon, but left out the sugar."

"Iced tea sounds wonderful, and dinner sounds wonderful, Emma. We can make a salad with the watermelon, bananas and cottage cheese."

"I'll make it," Emma said. "You just relax, visit with your granddaddy, and enjoy what's left of this fine August day. I'll have some munchies for you in a minute. Had everything ready an hour ago."

After Emma had gone into the house, Wes said, "You said you had an eventful day at the clinic, and I know *that* look. Something's up. I also heard you leave the house around four this morning."

"We had an emergency, Grandfather. A dog had a bone wedged in his trachea, and we had to remove it surgically."

"And?"

Jennifer couldn't meet her grandfather's eyes. "The dog is going to be fine, and we gave the owner the usual lecture regarding bones."

"Uh-huh. Doesn't sound that eventful to me. Oh, I know every surgery can be life threatening, but you've been trained to handle emergencies, and with Ben's expertise . . ."

Emma returned to the porch with a plate filled with carrot sticks, radishes and celery. "Guess you know I'd give anything for a bowl of potato chips and some onion dip," she said with a sigh.

Jennifer grinned. "I know, but just keep looking at yourself in the mirror, Emma. You look wonderful."

Emma flushed rosy pink, helped herself to a stalk of celery, and sat down.

Wes took a bite of carrot before he said, "Jennifer was just going to tell me about her 'eventful' day, Emma. They performed surgery on a dog that had a bone stuck in its throat."

"Stuck in the trachea, or windpipe," Jennifer said, "but that wasn't the end of it. The dog is okay, but . . ."

Wes nodded his head. "Now we get to the good part."

"Ben thought it was a chicken bone, but . . ."

Emma scowled. "But—but what?"

Jennifer took a deep breath. "It wasn't a chicken bone. It was one of the phalanges—finger bones, of a human hand."

Emma sucked in her breath, and Wes shook his head.

Jennifer went on. "Ben took the bone to the hospital to be analyzed. As you know, they don't have a forensic lab over there, but the technicians always seem to be on top of things. They verified my suspicions. Ben took the bone to the sheriff, and then I questioned the dog's owner. I didn't tell him it was a human bone, of course. I simply asked him if he knew where the dog had gotten the bone. He didn't. The dog runs a lot, and last night he was gone a couple of hours. When he came home, he was having trouble breathing."

"And the owner?" Emma asked.

"His name is Dan Wise. He works at the dairy and lives in one of the company cottages."

Wes scrunched up his face. "Elmer Dodd, huh? You suppose the dog found the bone on his property?"

Emma was sitting on the edge of her chair now,

and her eyes were very bright. "Lordy, wouldn't *that* be something!"

Jennifer shook her head. "You read too many mysteries, Emma."

"*I* read too many mysteries? Now where do you suppose I get them? You must have every mystery novel ever published stuffed on the shelves in the library."

"And you enjoy them as much as I do," Jennifer said with a grin. "But as far as Elmer Dodd is concerned, I think it's just a coincidence the dog's owner happens to work for him, and lives in one of his cottages. The dog was gone for two hours, and could have covered the whole town in that length of time."

"Which means that somewhere around town, we've got us a human skeleton," Wes reasoned. "Good Lord, what next?"

"That's basically what Ben and Nettie said. I know it's a scary thought, and conjures up all sorts of bizarre images."

"Is there any way to tell how long a person has been dead by a small section of bone?" Wes asked thoughtfully.

"I'm sure there is, and I plan to talk to the sheriff about it in the morning. Meanwhile, you have no idea how good it is to be home. Everywhere I went today, I kept looking down at the ground, expecting to see another bone from a finger, or worse.''

Wes reached over and squeezed Jennifer's hand. ''I'm glad you're home, too, sweetheart. At least when you're here, we know you're safe and sound.''

''I'll second that,'' Emma said stoutly, but she looked deep in thought. ''Indian bones,'' she said finally, smoothing down the skirt of her print housedress. ''There were a lot of Fox Indians around these parts years ago. Maybe the dog found an Indian burial ground. Lordy, that would be something! Or maybe it was some old trapper or fur trader from years gone by. Back in those days, people got killed at the blink of an eye, and a lot of 'em never got a proper burial. Just tossed the bodies out in a gully, shoveled a little dirt over 'em, and went on with business.''

Wes nodded. ''That's good, sound reasoning, Emma, and more than likely the answer. Could be the recent storm uncovered the remains.''

Jennifer listened to them discuss all the possibilities until dinner was ready, but didn't have the heart to tell them they were overlooking one other viable explanation: It was a modern-day crime. Somebody had killed somebody, and buried the body in a shallow grave.

Or maybe they were thinking it and just didn't

want to say it, because all through dinner they kept exchanging curious glances, and only picked at their food.

Jennifer tried to make light of it by complimenting Emma on the meal, the bouquet of yellow roses on the dining-room table, and discussing the weather, how fall was just around the corner, but nothing seemed to take them out of their doldrums.

Finally, Wes sat back in his chair, placed his fingers together in a pyramid, and said, "Guess there's no point in trying to hide how I feel, sweetheart. Let the sheriff handle this. I know you feel like you're in the middle of it because of the circumstances, but there isn't anybody in town who wouldn't understand if you sat this one out."

Emma spoke up. "You're granddaddy is trying to tell you he's worried. You're a veterinarian, and that's what you should be doing. We know you have a keen mind for this sort of thing, but you've only been home a few months, and you've already been in more trouble than a decent body has a right to be in. And don't tell us not to worry. Can't help that any more than breathing."

Jennifer finished the last of the watermelon on her plate, and sighed. "And I can't help becoming involved, any more than breathing. Seems to me we had this same conversation before I went off to college."

"Only because we were aware of how easily you could get sidetracked," Wes said.

Emma scoffed. "That's just a way of saying you were always getting into trouble, and that hasn't changed."

Wes shook his head. "You're an adult, and I shouldn't be telling you how to live your life."

Jennifer gave him a warm smile. "No, you shouldn't, but I understand. Only . . ."

Emma clucked her tongue. "Only you aren't going to change. Guess we wouldn't want you to. I've got some frozen yogurt in the freezer, if anybody wants some."

They ate dishes of frozen yogurt on the porch, watched fireflies dance in the moonlight while stars blinked on and off in the sky, and talked about everything except the bone, and the rest of the elusive skeleton. But it wasn't out of their thoughts. Not for one minute, and it wouldn't be until they had some answers, because no matter how worried her grandfather and Emma were— and she loved them for their concern—their minds were just as creative as hers.

*   *   *

Jennifer was waiting for the sheriff when he arrived at his office the following morning. He looked frazzled, as though he hadn't had much sleep, and she could certainly empathize, because she'd spent a restless night too, tossing and turning.

"Sorry we couldn't connect yesterday," he said, heading for the coffeepot, "but it was late when I got back to town. Didn't find any trace of the rustlers, so the whole day was wasted." He poured two cups of coffee, handed one to Jennifer, and scowled. "Nettie gave me the message. So the dog's owner has no idea where he got the bone?"

"No, he doesn't, and the dog was gone for approximately two hours. Think about the area he could have covered, Sheriff. Because of that, I only have one suggestion. We'll have to wait until the dog has recovered from surgery, and then hope he leads us to the spot where he found the bone."

Nettie pursed her lips. "I think I saw a Disney movie like that once. Only it was a cat. A Siamese cat. Good guys were trying to find the bad guys. The cat knew where the bad guys were, and the good guys had to chase the cat all over town."

"*That Darn Cat!*" the sheriff said. It's one of my wife's favorite movies. Have it on videotape. Hayley Mills and Dean Jones. And yeah, I can see something like that happening. Don't much like it, though. We could spend a lot of hours and man-power on it, and come up empty-handed.''

''Do you have a better suggestion?'' Jennifer asked, walking over to the area map on the wall.

''You know I don't, Jennifer, so don't get smart.''

Jennifer smiled at him, and pointed at the map. ''Okay, the dairy is here. Southwest of town, and not too far from that awful plot of land Elmer Dodd tried to shove off on the senior citizens. Who owns the land in between?''

The sheriff shook his head. ''I don't know, but we can sure find out.''

Nettie raised a hand and picked up the phone.

While Nettie talked to the County Recorder at City Hall, Jennifer studied the map. ''The dairy is surrounded by open land, Sheriff. It would take us forever to search it all.''

''Uh-huh. Talk about your proverbial needle in a haystack. We can't do it, Jennifer, and I'm not even going to try.''

''Is there a way to tell how long a person has been dead by the bones?''

''Yeah, and a whole lot more. I've got a book around here that explains all that, but I think we'd have to have a good part of the skeleton to get that kind of information.''

"The book is on the shelf to your left, Sheriff," Nettie said. "Blue cover." She was off the phone, and literally smirked. "That plot of land belongs to Elmer Dodd."

"So he owns all the land between the dairy and the dumps," the sheriff said, looking at the map. "Sounds like he was thinking about expanding the dairy. Uh-huh, I've got the picture. He buys it, decides the land isn't even fit for the dairy, and lets it sit, until he volunteers a section of it for the senior citizens' center. What a creep."

"Creep doesn't quite cover it," Jennifer said. She had taken the book off the shelf, and was flipping through the pages. She shuddered when she reached the autopsy section with its bold, graphic photos, and finally found what she was looking for. *The Human Skeleton in Forensic Medicine.* And it didn't take very long for her to realize they couldn't do much with what they had.

But she still found the whole thing fascinating, and had gone through two cups of coffee before she finished the chapter. With enough of the skeleton, experts in the field, such as forensic specialists and physical anthropologists, could provide the victim's age, sex, race, height, and other individual characteristics. Teeth were important for identification, but even without them, if the experts had the skull, they could go into forensic sculpture, or facial reconstruction. And if, in fact, the sheriff was lucky enough to find enough of the skeleton, he could ship it off to the F.B.I. lab in Washington, D.C., and request a full-blown examination. The book even explained how to do the paperwork, and package the evidence for shipment via the U.S. Postal Service, registered mail.

The sheriff pointed at the book. "Don't have much use for all that fancy stuff around here, but now and again I read up on what I'd probably be doing if I was a cop in a big city."

Nettie snorted. "Sounds to me like the big city is coming to us, in more ways than one. And seems like that Wexler clan over at *The Calico Review* can't wait. They've been calling us every day for years, hoping for a bit of news to print, but now I can hear the tone in their voices. Eager anticipation. No other way to put it. Old John Wexler might not care, because he's still living in the Dark Ages, back when the paper wasn't much more than a few sheets stuffed with human interest stories and recipes, or whose kid cut a tooth, or whose corn grew the highest. But now that his son, John, Jr., is fresh out of college and in charge, things have changed. Jennifer can certainly attest to that, the way they've been splashing her name all over the front page. I'm surprised they aren't following her around with binoculars. Heaven help us if they get a hold of this. . . ."

"They might," Jennifer said thoughtfully. "I haven't exactly kept it a secret. Ben knows, of course, and my grandfather and Emma. And we can't forget the laboratory technicians at the hospital."

The sheriff grinned. "Ben said he didn't exactly put the fear of God in them, but he came close. Said it was official police business, so they'll keep quiet. Are you going to tell Willy?"

"Unless you don't want me to. I'm having lunch with him today at Kelly's Coffee Shop, and frankly, I don't see how I can keep it from him. He knows me too well. He'll take one look at my face, and then hound me to death until he finds out what kind of a mess I've gotten myself into this time. But Willy can be trusted, Sheriff, and might even have an opinion or two."

The sheriff nodded. "And we can use all the help we can get."

Jennifer looked at her watch, and gave the sheriff a sly grin. "I have to get to work. If I see any reporters following me, I'll run the other way."

"Yeah, well you might not know a reporter when you see one," the sheriff warned. "I've heard John, Jr., has hired a whole crew of sleuthing newspeople, and every one of them are out there, trying to make a name for themselves.''

Jennifer thought about that as she headed for the clinic, but she really wasn't surprised. Like everything else, the newspaper was trying to keep up with the times.

Kelly's Coffee Shop was nestled between Nancy's Sewing Nook and the pharmacy, and faced Lincoln Street Park. All three establishments shared a rear courtyard, though the coffee shop used up most of the space to handle the overflow of diners during the summer months. They had started with just a few patio tables and now had ten, and each was topped by a colorful, striped umbrella.

It had been a busy morning at the clinic, and Jennifer was ready for a welcome break. She found Willy sitting at a corner table near the rose arbor, reading a book.

''Big case?'' Jennifer teased, sitting down across from him.

He got up and gave her a hug. ''Yeah. A big-time attorney is defending a killer, who really isn't the killer at all. He's only pretending to be so they can catch the real killer.''

''Sounds convoluted to me.''

"It is, but it's still a good book. Makes me wonder what it would be like to live in a big city where things *really* happen."

Willy had brown curly hair and blue, blue eyes, and Jennifer adored him. She reached across the table and took his hand. "You sound like a friend I had in vet school, who couldn't understand why I wanted to go into practice in Calico. Said within six months I'd be so bored, I'd head for the 'big city where things *really* happen.' Little did she know. So my advice to you? Stick around if you *really* want to see things happen. Haven't you been reading the papers?"

Willy grinned. "Who has to read about it in the paper when I've got a direct line into the frenzied life and times of Jennifer Gray, who always seems to have the inside scoop on everything. So what's happening now? Don't tell me, let me guess. The bank was robbed, and you know where the bad guy is hiding out."

Jennifer laughed. "It might even be better than that." She lowered her voice, gave him a brief accounting, and then sat back and waited while he weighed the possibilities.

Finally, he said, "Maybe the dog uncovered an Indian burial ground."

"That's what Emma said. She also said it could

be some long-ago resident of Calico, like a trapper or fur trader. You know the history of our town. It was pretty wild back then. . . .''

A pretty waitress, who Jennifer had never seen before, approached the table to take their order. After she had gone, Willy said, ''Yeah, it was pretty wild back then, but what *if*?''

''That's right, what *if*? What if somebody was murdered recently, buried the body, and the storm uncovered the bones? It would be a much more reasonable explanation.''

''And scarier. That would mean we have a killer running around Calico.''

''We have to find more of the skeleton, Willy, so the sheriff can send the remains to the F.B.I. in Washington.''

Willy shook his head. ''Bet they'll be glad to hear from us again! It wasn't all that long ago the Feds were called in because of that double kidnapping. They spent a lot of hours on that, and when they found out that Jennifer, along with some local help, had solved the case, they were pretty miffed. They've probably got a big sign nailed to their bulletin board in Washington that says, 'If anybody from Calico, Nebraska, calls, hang up'!''

''But this is different, Willy. Even more serious.''

"What if the rest of the skeleton isn't found?"

"Think positive, Willy. That would mean we'd have an unsolved mystery on our hands, and that's a scary thought, too."

"What about missing persons? Wouldn't the sheriff have a record of that sort of thing?"

"I'm sure he does, but I would think if somebody was really missing, the whole town would know about it, by way of *The Calico Review*, if nothing else."

A few minutes later, the waitress brought their chef salads and iced tea to the table, and a few minutes after that, Willy swallowed the piece of lettuce he was chewing, and said, "Uh-oh. The sheriff just walked in, and I don't think he's here to have lunch."

Jennifer turned around and waved, but the sheriff was already headed for their table.

"Hate to bother you," the sheriff said, "but thought you'd want to know . . ." He looked at Willy. "Did she tell you?" When Willy nodded, the sheriff pulled up a chair and sat down. "We've got ourselves another bone. Some boys found it. They thought it was an animal bone, and took it home. Bottom line, the parents thought it looked like a human bone, and brought it to me."

Jennifer felt a sudden chill. "And?"

"Well, I haven't taken it to the lab, you understand, but I'd say it's human. I compared it with the photos in that book you were looking at this morning, Jennifer, and I'd say it's the hip joint."

Willy whistled through his teeth. "Did the boys say where they found it?"

"Yeah, and this is the good part. Was near a sinkhole on the land Elmer Dodd owns next to the dairy, so it looks as though that section he donated to the senior citizens isn't the only plot of land crumbling into oblivion."

"Have you been down to look at the spot?" Jennifer asked.

"No, but I sent a couple of deputies to keep watch until I can get there. Thought you might want to tag along. You can come too, Willy, if you can get away."

"The paperwork on my desk can wait, Sheriff. Whoa. A hip joint, huh? Wonder why the boys didn't find the rest of the skeleton."

"Well, thank God they didn't," Jennifer said, trying to choke down her salad. "Can't you just see the parents' reaction to that?"

Willy grinned. "And it isn't even Halloween."

"I was thinking more in terms of pure panic," the sheriff grumbled. "You kids finish your lunch, and I'll meet you there."

Chapter Three

Jennifer maneuvered the Jeep Cherokee over the bumpy, rutted road in front of the now defunct senior citizens' center, and decided it was a miracle that there hadn't been more injuries when the roof collapsed. It had been almost a month since it happened, and yet nobody had bothered to clean up the rubble. The sight of it, and the deserted plot of land, bordered on the east by the waste disposal site, brought on an unexpected shudder. Dust rose above the area as bulldozers worked to cover the garbage of every Calico resident, and vultures circled overhead, making it even worse. To the west, beyond the expanse of land where the boys had found the bone, a row of tall cedar trees planted for a windbreak bordered the dairy.

54

It was the only vegetation around, and looked like an oasis.

Jennifer continued on until she reached the sheriff's patrol car, and pulled in beside it. She could barely see the sheriff in the distance, and finally said, "Can't we drive the rest of the way in? I mean, why did he park out here?"

"This whole area is probably riddled with sink-holes just waiting to open up," Willy said, adjusting the sunglasses on the bridge of his nose. "So I'm sure the sheriff parked here as a safety precaution." He gave her a lopsided grin. "You're the exercise nut. So what's a little walk?"

"I have no objections to taking a 'little walk,' " Jennifer said, climbing out of the Jeep. "It's just this place. It's so awful, and now with the discovery of the bone, and the circling vultures, suggesting something might be dead . . ." She shuddered again.

Willy walked around the Jeep and took her hand. "Come on, Jenny. Now isn't the time to get cold feet."

"I've never had cold feet in my life," she said, as they made their way over the uneven, dusty terrain. "Well, maybe once or twice, but I can't help the way I feel. It really is a terrible part of town. That's why I was so upset over the senior citizens' center. Can you imagine looking out a window at this?''

Willy grinned. ''Don't forget the wafting scents of cows and garbage.''

Jennifer groaned, and hurried her steps.

As they approached the sheriff, it was easy to see the excitement on his face. He'd removed his hat and tie, and perspiration soaked the front of his olive-green shirt.

''Sorry we're late,'' Jennifer said, ''but I wanted to tell Ben what was happening, and Willy wanted to change out of his suit into jeans and boots.''

''Good place for jeans and boots. That's Deputy Manny Pressman digging around in the sinkhole.''

Manny Pressman had taken off his shirt, and had a bandanna tied around his forehead as a sweatband. He looked up and grinned. ''We tossed a coin, and I lost.''

The sheriff chuckled. ''My infamous two-headed coin. Had another deputy with me at the beginning of this, but had to send him off on a call. Too bad, because he's missing all the fun. Take a look.'' He walked over to a large square of folded plastic near the sinkhole, and flipped it back.

Jennifer stared down at the large bone, and felt nauseous. "It looks like a femur, or thigh-bone. . . ."

"Uh-huh, that's my guess. For sure, it isn't a dog bone."

"Holy moly," Willy said, squatting down for a closer look.

The sheriff wiped his forehead with a handker-chief. "I know how you feel. When Manny held it up, I couldn't believe what I was seeing. I think an animal must've removed the bone the kids found from the sinkhole, or they would've even-tually found the skeleton."

"Where is the hip joint?" Jennifer asked, breathlessly.

"At the office with the first bone. Nettie is guarding them with her life."

Jennifer looked around the arid plot of land, and asked, "How many sinkholes are there?"

"Six. We picked this one because we could see where the kids had been digging a few feet away. I figure an animal partially buried the bone, and it was the kids' prize for the taking. You can see where they were digging deeper, trying to find more."

"What causes a sinkhole?" Jennifer asked.

The sheriff shrugged. "It's hard to say. Could

be natural corrosion. Maybe underground fissures. Could even be an underground stream, and because the sinkholes seem to form a line, I'd say that's a good possibility. Then, too, the ground has had time to dry out since the storm, but see all that seepage down at the bottom? Seems to me the dumps had a problem like this a few years back. But then I don't suppose it mattered much. If a sinkhole opens up over there, they fill it full of garbage and bulldoze it over.''

Jennifer pressed on. ''What about the dairy? Any complaints from Elmer Dodd about sinkholes?''

''No complaints from Dodd that I know of.''

''Shouldn't we be helping the deputy?'' Willy asked.

''One person tramping around down there at a time is enough, Willy. Otherwise, we could do more harm than good.''

A few minutes later, Manny let out a hoot, and held up several smaller bones. ''They look like rib bones, Sheriff, and I've uncovered a whole pile of round bones. Maybe part of the spine.''

As repulsive as it was, Jennifer found her pulse quicken. ''Does it sound ghoulish to admit I'm excited?'' she finally managed to get out.

The sheriff grinned. ''Hell, no. This is a monumental break, Jennifer. And we can thank those kids. If they hadn't found that bone, we'd be all over the countryside, getting nowhere, or sitting around twiddling our thumbs, getting nowhere.''

The sinkhole was approximately six feet deep and ten feet in diameter, and the walls were at an angle, allowing for easy access. Jennifer watched the deputy bring up the bones and place them on the sheet of plastic. With a sigh, she said, ''You know it's only going to be a matter of time before the media gets wind of this. The kids found the bone, the parents thought it looked like a human bone, and nobody swore them to secrecy.''

The sheriff shrugged. ''Not much we can do about that. About all we can do is keep the area cordoned off, which will tell everybody it's official police business, and keep a deputy on guard at all times, so we won't have half the town down here digging things up. If we don't handle it that way, it could end up a zoo. Meanwhile, let them think what they want. Our lips are sealed, and will be until we get the report back from the Feds.''

''And if it's a homicide?''

''Then we've got ourselves a full-blown investigation ahead of us.''

Willy spoke up. ''Jennifer and I discussed this at lunch, Sheriff. Have you had any calls regarding a missing person, other than the case with the two Peterson boys recently?''

"Nope. Oh, we had a missing husband a couple of years ago, who turned up in the backroom at the roadhouse sleeping it off; and June Frank went to visit her sister in Omaha and forgot to leave her husband a note, but other than that, we haven't had a missing person in years.''

"Well, it has to be *somebody*,'' Jennifer said.

"What about an Indian burial ground?'' Willy asked. "Do you think that's a possibility?''

The sheriff sighed. "Well, I'd rather believe that than the fact I have a homicide on my hands. But I've gotta tell you, if this was an Indian burial ground, we should be finding Indian artifacts along with the bones, because those people were always buried with their possessions. For sure, we should find more than one body. Can't say we still won't, but we sure haven't found any Indian artifacts.''

For the next hour, while Willy hiked the property checking out the rest of the sinkholes, Jennifer watched Manny Pressman uncover bone after bone. And by the time Willy returned, they were very close to having a complete skeleton, and a lot more. Manny had uncovered *three* thighbones, and several extra pieces.

Willy took off his shirt, wiped the perspiration from his brow with the bottom of his T-shirt, and pointed at the bones that had been placed on the sheet of plastic. "That's a damned grisly sight."

Jennifer nodded, trying to hold in her excitement. "We're still missing quite a few bones, but the sheriff seems to think we have more than enough to send to Washington. Now, how about taking a closer look."

Willy stepped up for a closer look, and then let out a gasp. "Holy moly! *Two* skeletons?"

Jennifer grinned. "That's right. Can you believe it?"

"And not one sign of Indian artifacts," the sheriff said, with a woebegone expression. "So that tells me this is murder. Maybe even a double murder."

Willy shoved his hands in the pockets of his jeans, and kicked at a rock. "I hate to bring this up, but I take it you haven't found the skulls?"

"No, we haven't," the sheriff said. "And that's why we're going to keep digging. We have enough to send to the Feds, but I'd sure like to send along a skull or two. We haven't a chance of getting a positive I.D. without them."

Willy went on, "Well, I think you were right about the underground stream. I found a stream near the trees bordering the back end of the dairy. It goes into a culvert and then disappears, but it's in line with the sinkholes here and next-door. Probably continues on underground, right through the dumps, and that's why they've had problems in the past. It isn't much more than a trickle where it goes into the culvert, but I could see the high-water marks further up. Must have overflowed its banks during the storm. And if you look close, in between the sinkholes, you'll find the soil a little softer. That's probably why the culprit decided to bury the bodies here. Otherwise, he would've had to dig through hardpan. Yikes, *two* skeletons! Any tire tracks?''

Willy's reaction brought a smile to the sheriff's face. "No tire tracks, and that's what I call good investigating, Willy. You ever get tired of being a lawyer, let me know."

At that moment, movement caught Jennifer's eye. She turned, and sucked in her breath. It was John Wexler, Jr., who was now managing editor of *The Calico Review*. Quite an undertaking for a twenty-two-year-old kid just out of college, who thought he was God's gift to journalism. He was still some distance away, but it was easy to see by his straight shoulders and broad strides he was excited. It was the demeanor of any reporter who was on the threshold of a big story. John Wexler, Sr., had founded the newspaper, and John, Jr., had inherited his father's arrogance and tenacity. He had never been a part of her circle of friends because of their difference in age, but he'd always managed to make his presence felt.

Jennifer quickly scooped up both shirts, jumbled the bones into a smaller pile, and covered them with the shirts before she muttered, "We have company, Sheriff. It's John, Jr., and he's walking like a man with a purpose."

Manny scrambled out of the sinkhole, brushed off his pants, and grumbled, "I wonder who tipped him off?"

"Maybe the kids' parents," Willy reasoned. "Want me to handle it?"

"I'll handle it," Jennifer said. "He has always been a jerk, and I have the feeling he would do anything for a story."

The sheriff winked at Willy. "She's ticked because of all that stuff John's been putting in the newspaper about her."

Jennifer squared her shoulders. "You bet I'm ticked. From the day I stepped off the plane from Michigan, I've been fair game for his personal opinions, and that's bad journalism. *The Calico*

Review is supposed to be a newspaper, not a gossipy tabloid.''

Jennifer turned as the young man approached, and pasted a smile on her face. He was wearing tan slacks and a crisp white shirt, and every golden blond hair on his head was in place. He was quite handsome, and knew it. "Hello, John," she said crisply. "What brings you all the way out here?"

He mopped his brow with a handkerchief and scowled. "More to the point, what are *you* doing here?"

"Helping the sheriff check out the sinkholes."

He made a quick appraisal of the scene before his eyes settled on Willy. "Slow day in court, counselor?" he said finally.

Willy chose his words carefully before he said, "Slow day at the newspaper?"

John managed a smile. "Touché." He pointed at the sinkhole. "Is that where the kids found the bone?"

The sheriff stepped up. "Sounds like you've been talking to the parents. Well, I'll admit they've got good imaginations, but I'm sorry to say the bone turned out to be nothing more than a part of an animal. Probably a stray cow from the dairy, so I guess you've messed up your fancy shoes and nice tan pants for nothing.''

John looked down at his dust-covered clothing before he mocked, ''I don't think so. If the bone was from a cow, why are you out here digging around? Oh, right, you're checking out the sinkholes. Mind if I ask why?''

''Don't mind at all,'' the sheriff said easily. ''We've counted six sinkholes, and there could be a lot more, just waiting to open up. That makes this a dangerous area, young man, so as the Sheriff of Peace County . . .''

John picked up a shovel and leaned on the handle. ''Cut the bull, Sheriff. Two shovels, and from the looks of your deputy, he's been doing a lot of digging. Why don't you just come clean? The town has a right to know what's going on. Elmer Dodd has a right to know what's going on. I suppose he knows you're poking around on his property?''

The sheriff's smile turned into a scowl. He told Manny to get the Mylar tape and stakes out of his patrol car, and faced John Wexler. ''Okay, I'll cut the bull, Wexler. This is a dangerous area, and you're interfering with official police business. As of this moment, I'm cordoning off the area. Print what you want, but facts are facts.''

John grinned. "Official police business? Then it *was* a human bone."

"I didn't say that."

"You didn't have to."

John's eyes were roaming again, and finally settled on the two shirts stretched out on the ground. They covered the plastic and bones well enough, but seemed so obvious to Jennifer, she held her breath, waiting for him to ask what they had hidden under the shirts. But he didn't. He simply turned around and walked away, but not before she caught the malevolent smile on his face.

Willy took a deep breath. "I hate to say it, Sheriff, but he's going to cause trouble."

The sheriff nodded. "I know, but he can't do much without proof. And I meant what I said. I'm cordoning off the area, and I'll keep a deputy here at all times. God knows, I can't afford to lose the manpower, but I don't have a choice. This is too important. I'm sending what we have to Washington first thing in the morning."

"And the skulls?" Jennifer asked.

"We'll keep digging."

"And Elmer Dodd? How are you going to explain this to him?"

"I have the feeling Wexler is gonna do that for me. All I can do is stick to my story. It's a police matter, official business, and the fact that it's happening on Dodd's property is the basic issue. He doesn't have the property fenced, or any signs posted, and that should keep him in line. But you know, I don't think he'd put up much of a fuss anyway. He just went through a mess with the senior citizens, and he couldn't stand another controversy, not when he has his eyes set on the mayor's big old desk and comfortable chair.'' He looked at his watch. ''You kids might as well head on back to town. The rest of my deputies have been instructed to meet me here, and I want to have a powwow about security before it gets too late.''

''Do you want us to help package up the bones for shipment?'' Jennifer asked.

The sheriff nodded. ''That's gonna fall on Nettie's shoulders, so I'm sure she'd appreciate your help. First time for something like this, you know, and she's gonna be in a tizzy. And to tell you the truth, the sooner it gets done, the better, because I sure don't like the idea of having a pile of human bones lying around the office.'' He scratched his head. ''Don't much like the idea of leaving them in the office overnight, either, even if they are boxed up. Guess I'll sleep on the cot in the storeroom. I'll tell my wife I'm baby-sitting some important evidence, and let it go at that.''

"Then you didn't tell her about the first bone?" Jennifer asked.

"Didn't see any point in getting her all riled up before we knew what we had. As it is, she thinks the town is going straight to hell. Now, with things going from bad to worse . . . she thinks I should retire. . . .'' He rubbed his fingers across his eyes. "Guess it doesn't matter much now, though. Wexler is gonna print it up in the paper, and the whole town, along with my wife, is gonna know what he thinks by morning.''

The sheriff watched Manny Pressman dump the roll of yellow Mylar tape, stakes and a hammer out of a duffel bag, and sighed again. "You two might as well take the bones to the office and get started on that end of it. You can use the duffel bag to transport them. By the way, I haven't thanked you. You've been a big help.''

Jennifer gave the sheriff a hug. "We haven't done much except give you moral support, Sheriff, and we should be thanking you for letting us be a part of it. It means a lot.''

"It means a lot?" Willy said, after they were on their way back to town. "I'm an attorney, and you're a vet, Jenny. We have no business poking our noses into something like this.''

Willy had the duffel bag full of bones in his lap, and she gave it a pat. ''The sheriff trusts us, Willy, and that means a lot. And this is our town, and that means a lot. And if the sheriff needs our help, that means a lot, too.'' She looked over at him. ''You didn't have to come along this afternoon. And you don't have to go with me now. I'll take you back to your office, and—''

Willy raised his hand, as if to ward off her blows. ''Whoa, Jenny, relax. I wanted to go, and I'm willing to give a helping hand. Better that than letting you go off and do your own thing, while I worry myself sick.''

''Then don't complain.''

''I'm not complaining. This is my town, too, and I don't like the idea of having a killer on the loose any more than you do.''

Jennifer shivered. ''Well, let's keep our fingers crossed Emma is right. Let's hope we've uncovered the skeletons of a couple of old trappers or fur traders, and that they are at least a hundred years old.''

Willy nodded, but she could see the look in his eyes. He didn't believe it was going to be that easy, any more than she did.

Chapter Four

Jennifer knew something was wrong the minute she walked into the kitchen the following morning. Emma was whipping up waffle batter for one thing, and her grandfather, who always took a shower and changed his clothes immediately after his jog to the river, was still wearing his dark blue warmups. And their faces! Glum, to say the least. Not even the sunlight filtering through the yellow curtains at the window, or the bouquet of purple asters on the table could brighten the mood.

And then she saw the morning newspaper, propped up against the silver coffee carafe at the end of the table, and knew what had happened. She sat down across from her grandfather, and sighed. "Do I dare ask?"

Wes sighed, too, and filled his cup with coffee. "When you called last night to say you'd be home late, we assumed you were at the clinic. But now we figure you must have been with the sheriff. Coffee?"

Jennifer nodded. "I didn't want to worry you, Grandfather. Not that I wasn't going to tell you about it. I just didn't want to do it over the phone."

Emma turned around and waved a wooden spoon. "Worry is having to read about it in the paper, young lady."

"You know better than to believe everything you read in the paper, Emma," Jennifer said defensively. "John, Jr., is just trying to stir up trouble. He hasn't a clue as to what's really going on."

"So would you like to tell us what's *really* going on?" Wes asked.

"Maybe I'd better read the lies in the paper first, and go from there."

Wes handed her the paper, muttering, "You're not going to like it."

Not surprised to see the bold headline across the front page declaring: WHO BURIED THE BONES? Jennifer read John Wexler's preposterous tale of murder and mayhem:

The sun was hot. Perspiration trickled down my back as I made my way across the barren, rut-filled ground. It was hard to breathe; the dust thick. At the time, I found myself thinking it would be a good place for a killer to bury a body. Right in the middle of twenty acres of nothing. Twenty desolate acres. What drew me out to that forlorn section of town in the first place? The cries of a nearly hysterical mother whose young sons had found a bone while playing a simple game of cowboys and Indians. They took it home to their parents who in turn took it to the sheriff, because they thought it looked like a human bone. We can only venture a guess as to what happened after that, but it is my professional opinion we are in the middle of some kind of a murder investigation, and once again, mystery and intrigue hangs like a black shroud over our peaceful town of Calico.

But let me go on with my harrowing, chilling experience.

As I drew closer and closer to the spot, I could see I wasn't alone. The sheriff was already there with one of his deputies. Interestingly enough, Jennifer Gray and attorney Willy Ashton were there, too, which immediately put me on alert. Trouble seems to follow Jennifer Gray around like a well-trained puppy. Or perhaps it's the other way around. One has to wonder how she finds the time to work at the animal clinic.

And we all know Willy. His keen, legal mind is always sharp and alert to anything that might lead to a courtroom battle.

In any event, it was obvious to me they had been doing some serious digging, but they refused to share in their findings. Nor was I welcome. I was told by the sheriff the bone in question was an animal bone, but in the next breath, I was told the area was being cordoned off, and that I was interfering with police business. Now, you tell me, folks. Doesn't that sound like a cover-up to you? And don't you believe, as I do, that we have a right to the truth? Police business aside, if somebody has been murdered, we must ban together to protect ourselves from the evil hands of the killer.

"Well, he didn't exactly lie," Jennifer said, shoving the newspaper aside. But I can't believe all the melodramatics. He should be a novelist instead of trying to run a newspaper.

Emma let out a *hr-rump*. "He'd make a bad book writer, too."

"Then everything he said was true?" Wes asked, filling his cup with coffee again.

Jennifer wanted to tell her grandfather he was drinking too much coffee, and she wanted to tell Emma to toss the waffle batter down the sink and fix a nutritious breakfast, but she couldn't do either one. They were upset, and there were definitely times when a bit of solace could be found in rib-sticking food. She wanted a waffle too, with lots of butter and syrup, and at least three cups of coffee. "Yes," she said finally. "It basically happened the way he described, without the theatrics, but he really doesn't know anything, and that's what has him upset. It's just a lot of speculation. Unfortunately, he's a lot closer than he thinks."

Wes took a deep breath. "So you found the rest of the skeleton?"

"The deputy uncovered two skeletons, Grandfather. . . ."

"Good gosh," Emma said, heaving a sigh.

"Willy and I were having lunch yesterday at Kelly's Coffee Shop when the sheriff walked in with the news. Some boys playing near a sinkhole on the plot of land between the defunct senior citizens' center and the dairy found a bone. They took it home to their parents, the parents thought it looked like a human bone, and took it to the sheriff. The sheriff didn't say anything to the parents, of course, but he compared it with some photographs in one of his books, and decided it was a hip joint. Willy and I went down to the site, and by mid-afternoon, a good portion of both skeletons had been exhumed. That's when John, Jr., showed up.''

Emma said, "How did he find out about it?''

"From John's running narrative in the paper, I'd say the boys' parents took the story to the newspaper, after they took the bone to the sheriff. Maybe even to John, Jr., himself, and that was all he needed. Willy and the deputy had removed their shirts, and when I saw John, Jr., coming, I used the shirts to cover the bones. But my heart was up in my throat the whole time, because I just knew *he* knew what we were trying to hide. Well, maybe he did, maybe he didn't, but he was very suspicious, and alluded to the fact he knew all about the human bone the boys had found. The sheriff told him it was an animal bone, but John, Jr., didn't buy it. Before it was over, the sheriff told John, Jr., he was going to cordon off the area, and that he was interfering with official police business. I know it was the wrong thing to say, because it simply verified John's suspicions, but the sheriff didn't have a choice. And he did cordon off the area, and has made plans to keep a deputy on duty at the site until we have some answers. Of course they could be the skeletons of some long-ago residents, as Emma suggested before, but until we know . . .''

"So how do you find out?" Emma asked, fanning her face with her apron. "Lordy, *two* skeletons. That's even worse than a dead body."

"The bones are being sent to the F.B.I. in Washington, D.C., with instructions to conduct a full examination. The sheriff should have results in about a week, if they get right on it. That's why I got home so late last night. Willy and I helped Nettie package up the bones. What a nightmare! The sheriff has a book full of instructions, because it has to be done a certain way, and talk about the paperwork! Poor Nettie was pulling out her hair."

"Speaking of hair, what about the skulls?" Wes asked.

Emma sucked in her breath. "Mr. Wes!"

"Well, it seems to me, without the skulls, they won't get very far."

"We didn't find the skulls, Grandfather, and you're right. Without them, they won't be able to identify the bodies. But they will be able to tell if they are male or female, the approximate age at death, how long they've been dead, and some physical characteristics, such as height and race. If we're lucky, they'll even be able to tell us how they died."

"Sounds like those old *Quincy* stories to me," Emma snorted, pouring batter into the waffle iron.

"What it is, is modern-day police work, Emma, and it's really quite remarkable."

"Does Donald Attwater still own that plot of land?" Wes asked.

"Mayor Attwater? No, Elmer Dodd owns it, and I don't imagine he's going to be too thrilled with this. But like the sheriff says, he probably won't kick up a fuss because he can't afford another controversy."

Emma scoffed, "And finding a couple of skeletons on his property isn't controversial?"

Wes shook his head. "What I find controversial, or maybe 'questionable' would be a better word, is the fact Elmer Dodd actually bought that plot of land. You would think he'd learned his lesson when he bought the plot next to the dumps. Not good for a solitary thing."

"Maybe he bought the two plots at the same time," Jennifer reasoned. "Or maybe he was thinking ahead, to a time when the town is so big, the waste disposal site will have to be expanded. Then he could sell it to the town for a healthy profit. As it stands now, that's exactly what he plans to do."

Emma frowned. "Then why did he donate it to the senior citizens in the first place?"

"I think he saw it as a chance to make some

kissy points because he plans to run for mayor next year. And maybe he bought the other plot of land because he had plans to expand the dairy.''

Wes nodded. "Makes sense. Now, tell me about the sinkholes, Jennifer. That whole area seems to be riddled with them, and I find that very curious indeed. Sounds like there might be some kind of an underground stream.''

Jennifer nodded. "The sheriff and Willy are sure of it. Willy found a stream behind the dairy. It empties into a culvert and then disappears. The sinkholes sort of snake along between both properties.''

"Uh-huh, following the stream. Years of corrosion. The last storm was probably the last straw.''

"And it's possible the stream extends into the waste disposal site because the sheriff said they had problems with sinkholes a few years back. Do you suppose Mayor Attwater knew about the underground stream when he sold the property to Elmer Dodd?''

"I doubt it. Donald might be a bit lazy, and even scatterbrained at times, but I think he's an honorable man.'' Wes pointed at the paper. "Speaking of honorable men, did you notice how young John Wexler comes close to being slanderous, and then stops short? He didn't come right out and accuse you of not doing your job as a vet, he simply suggested it must be hard for you to find the time. And Willy. Read between the lines, and he's saying Willy would do just anything for a case. Makes me wonder why he didn't print the fact the property belongs to Elmer Dodd. Or maybe he doesn't know who it belongs to.''

''He knows, because he mentioned Elmer Dodd's name. Said he wondered how Dodd was going to like us snooping around on his property. But the title is a matter of public record, and any reporter with his feet on the ground would have checked that out, first thing. And even though he didn't mention Dodd in the paper, he gave enough of a description to pen down the location, if anybody has a mind to. I have the feeling it's only a matter of time before the area is going to turn into a muddle of looky-loos and curiosity seekers. The sheriff was afraid of that happening, and I'm sure he's expecting it.''

''So now what?'' Wes asked.

''The sheriff is going to keep looking for the skulls, keep the area cordoned off and guarded, and wait for the lab results from Washington.''

''Along with fighting off the folks in town who will take young John, Jr.'s, word as gospel, and demand answers,'' Emma said, placing a waffle in front of Jennifer. ''You didn't tell me to toss the batter down the sink, so I figured you might be wanting one too. Maple syrup or berry?''

''Maple . . .''

Wes grinned. ''That'a girl, Jennifer. Every now and again a body needs comfort food, and this sure seems to be the morning for it.''

It was also the morning for questions, and by the time Jennifer was on her way to the clinic, she had a dozen of them listed in her head.

''The phone has been ringing off the hook,'' Ben said, when Jennifer walked through the back door.

Jennifer looked at her watch. ''It's only eight-thirty, Ben. What's wrong with everybody? They know we don't open the clinic until nine.''

''Take a look at the appointment book, and then you tell me. I've had calls from people who don't have pets wanting to make an appointment. Even had one lady waiting on the stoop when I opened up, demanding to talk to you.''

''Oh, oh. John, Jr.'s, story in the morning paper must have caught their attention.''

''I'd say it did more than catch their attention.''

''Did you read it?''

"I did, and I also read between the lines. I figured you must have found more bones on the property, Wexler showed up, and you had a genuine free-for-all."

Jennifer slipped into her lab coat. "Well, it wasn't exactly a free-for-all, but it was enough to upset him. But basically what he said is true, if you can wade through the theatrics. He just doesn't know *everything*. Deputy Pressman uncovered enough to ship to Washington, but there's more. He found two skeletons, Ben, and it's looking more and more like murder."

"Whoa. That's a shock."

"I know. The sheriff hasn't found the skulls yet, but at least it's a start."

"I take it Wexler didn't see the bones?"

"No. They were covered up. And then when the sheriff told John, Jr., he was interfering with official police business . . ."

Jennifer's words were cut off by the ringing phone, and she picked it up. "Calico Veterinary Clinic . . ."

"Is it true there has been a murder in Calico, and you know who the killer is?" the man's voice bellowed in her ear.

Jennifer took a deep breath. "This is a veterinary clinic, sir. If you'd like to make an appointment . . ."

"Don't want no damned appointment. I want some answers! I called the sheriff, and got his secretary. Boy, was that a joke. You people sure know how to jerk a person around. I moved to Calico to get away from all the bad stuff in the city, and . . ."

"I'm sorry, sir," Jennifer interrupted, "but if you're not going to make an appointment, I'm afraid I'll have to hang up. You have a good day."

Ben sighed. "And I'm afraid you're in for a bit of a nightmare, Jennifer. Maybe you should take the day off."

Jennifer tossed her head. "I'm not going into hiding, Ben. But I'll let you in on a little secret. I could cheerfully strangle John, Jr. His little dramatic accounting is going to make all our lives miserable."

When the phone rang again, Ben took it, and then called the switchboard, instructing the operator to take all incoming calls. "I don't want a blasted call coming in that isn't an emergency," he told her, and his words were final.

But handling the flow of people wasn't as easy. By the time they were ready to unlock the front door at nine o'clock, the line outside was two abreast, and reached the road.

Jennifer peeked through the window and sighed. "We haven't room for them all, Ben, and half of them don't even have an animal. It's absolutely insane!"

Ben ran a weary hand over his eyes. "Do you have a suggestion?"

"Yes, I do, as a matter of fact. They might want to talk to me, but not any more than I want to talk to them! I'm going out, Ben."

"They'll swallow you up before you can get a foot on the porch."

"Then you get them off the porch, and tell them I'm coming out. Tell them I have an announcement to make."

Jennifer waited until Ben had cleared the porch, demanding silence, and then stepped out beside him. He took her hand, and she was grateful for that. She even put a smile on her face, though she felt like screaming. And the anger she could see on their faces was overwhelming. Some of the people she knew, but most of them were strangers, and that irked her the most of all. What right did they have to come here and confront her because of a piece of slipshod journalism?

She took a deep breath and began with, "If any

of you truly have an animal that must be looked at today, step off to one side.''

Several people moved off, but the rest stood firm. Jennifer continued. ''I'm sure most of you are here this morning because you read John Wexler's story in the paper. Unfortunately, he inferred that there is a murderer on the loose, and that I am part of a conspiracy to keep the residents of Calico in the dark. Well, it simply isn't true. Mr. Wexler is a newspaperman who has a vivid imagination.''

A man spoke up. ''Then can you tell us why the sheriff is digging up a plot of land south of town?''

''That plot of land is full of sinkholes, sir, and it's quite dangerous. Two little boys were playing there, and could have been badly injured. The sheriff has cordoned off the area for safety reasons, until he decides how to handle it. I would suspect that eventually the sinkholes will be filled in.''

The man smirked, ''Uh-huh, and didn't those boys find a bone in one of those sinkholes?''

Jennifer widened her smile. ''You mean the *human* bone Mr. Wexler alluded to in the paper? Apparently Mr. Wexler must have been having a slow day in the newsroom, and let his imagination flow. Anything to fill up space. I believe the bone was an animal bone, sir. And that's not at all unusual. For those of you who have lived here for any length of time, you know we have our fair share of coyotes, fox, and other critters roaming around the area, and bones are uncovered all the time. This is also cattle country, and many bleached bones can be found out on the prairie. I would suggest you all go home and think about that, as well as remember that Calico is a quiet, peaceful town. It's a nice place to live, and nothing can be garnered from fear. Sheriff Cody is a good man, and has all your interests at heart. And be assured. If there ever is a problem that puts the town in jeopardy, you will be the first to know.

''Now, this is a veterinary clinic, and we have a job to do. Give us a few minutes, and we'll open the door for business. As for the rest of you, I hope I've put your minds at ease.''

As the crowd began to disperse, Jennifer and Ben hurried inside. When the door was closed behind them, Ben muttered, ''This isn't going to be the end of it, Jennifer. I hope you realize that. Those people were only a small handful of residents, who have every right to be concerned. And as long as we have a man like John Wexler spreading rumors, unfounded or not, the folks are gonna stay stirred up.''

Jennifer lifted her chin. ''Then maybe I should go to the source, and have it out with John.''

''And make him agitated? He has the power of the press behind him, and you might find yourself facing a losing battle.''

''The power of the press, huh? Well, maybe that's the answer. Maybe I should write a letter to the editor, and let everybody know how I feel. Do you suppose he'd print it?''

''I think he'd have to, but I'd be careful. If the F.B.I. lab in Washington says it's murder, or worse, a double murder and it's recent, you might have to eat your words. If I were you, I'd let it go for now. And I'd stay out of it. Let the sheriff handle it.''

Jennifer gave Ben a hug. ''I'll try, Ben, but I can't promise. I have a jillion questions running around in my head, and I want answers. For example . . .''

Ben rolled his eyes, and raised a hand. ''Not now, Jennifer. Like you told all those good people, this is a veterinary clinic, and we have a job to do. It's time to open the door and get on with business.''

Jennifer headed for the door, but said over her

shoulder, ''For example, Mayor Attwater owned that horrid piece of land before he sold it to Elmer Dodd. Now Attwater is going to step down, and Elmer Dodd plans on running for mayor. From what I've heard, Attwater even plans on heading up the campaign. Don't you find that interesting?''

Ben groaned as Jennifer opened the door, and this time the smile on her face was very, very real.

Chapter Five

Curiously enough, it had ended up a rather slow day, and the work routine. And although Jennifer had to give an abbreviated version of her little speech several times to animal owners who needed reassurance, for the most part, she was met with understanding instead of hostility. Ben claimed it was her smiling face. It had been sweet of him, but it hadn't helped much. And then Elmer Dodd walked in, and everything changed. Something "dark and evil" wore a white linen suit, a Panama hat, and carried a long cigar. He looked like a villain on late-night TV instead of a businessman in Calico.

It was just before closing time, and Jennifer was straightening up the magazines in the waiting room when she heard the bells tinkle on the door. And although she wasn't surprised to see him, believing that he would seek her out sooner or later, she wasn't prepared, either. The best she could do was mutter, "You can't smoke in here, Mr. Dodd."

Elmer Dodd looked down at the cigar, shrugged, and flipped it out the door. When he was facing her again, he said, "Is Ben around?"

"Sorry, but you just missed him. He left a little early. . . ."

"I didn't come to see him, Jennifer. I came to see you. If I can have a few minutes of your time?"

Elmer Dodd was a short, portly man, with a large belly, bulbous nose, and dark, slicked-back hair. He also had yellow teeth and brown, beady eyes—it wasn't a pleasant picture. Nor was he pleasant to be around. She had a hard time with the fact he had actually gone to school with her father, because her father had been so handsome, and young and vital. And honest. Elmer Dodd didn't know the meaning of the word.

She had to restrain herself to keep from ordering him out, and tried a more tactful approach. "It's almost closing time, Mr. Dodd, and I'm expected home."

Elmer Dodd took off his hat, and perched on the edge of a straight-backed chair. "This won't take long. I tried talking to the sheriff, but got his usual brush-off. Now, I know John, Jr., over at *The Calico Review* has a vivid imagination, just like his daddy, and it's best to believe about half of what you read in the paper. But I do believe those two boys found a bone on my property, and I know for a fact the sheriff has cordoned off the area and has a deputy keeping watch. I tried to get through, down there where they're messing around, and was ordered off my own property. So the questions is, was it an animal bone or a human bone? Those boys' parents seem to think it's the latter, and that's why they took the bone to the sheriff.

"Now, if we can believe John, Jr., it's also a fact he found you and Willy Ashton, along with the sheriff and a deputy, digging up my property. That would suggest to me that you think it's a human bone, too, and as the owner of that property, I have the right . . ."

Jennifer took a deep breath. "As the owner of that property, you have every right in the world, Mr. Dodd, but as the sheriff of Peace County, Sheriff Cody has the right to keep the town out of harm's way. That plot of land is full of sinkholes, which makes it a very dangerous place indeed. For starters, the property isn't fenced, nor are there any warnings posted. Those two boys could have been seriously injured, and as the owner of the property, you would have been held responsible. I don't think I have to remind you what happened to the senior citizens' center. . . .''

His dark eyes narrowed. ''You're getting far afield here, Jennifer. What happened to the senior citizens' center has no bearing on this.''

''Of course it does, because that plot of land is full of sinkholes, too. Even if the roof hadn't collapsed, a sinkhole could have opened up, and taken the structure down. People could have been killed, and those boys could have been killed. And by the way, we weren't digging up your property. We were checking out the sinkholes. The sheriff simply cordoned off the area as a safety precaution.''

''Yeah? So why did the sheriff need you and Willy Ashton to help him 'check out' the sinkholes? And why did he ignore me when I told him I'd make arrangements to have all the sinkholes filled in? Told him I'd get a crew in from North Platte first thing tomorrow morning, but he wouldn't listen.''

Aware that her response could make or break

the conversation and, at the moment, it was vitally important to keep him pacified, Jennifer managed a smile. "Surely you understand that by simply filling in the sinkholes the problem won't be solved. Others can open up, and we're talking about a lot of acreage."

Elmer tapped his fingers on his knees. Finally, he said, "Then what do you suggest, Jennifer? You always seem to have all the answers."

He didn't mean it as a compliment, but she let it go. "Whatever happens is going to have to be the sheriff's decision, Mr. Dodd. But I do have one suggestion. Go have a little talk with John, Jr. He'll do more harm than good if he continues to print stories like the one he ran in the paper this morning. I call it shabby journalism, and the citizens of Calico deserve better than that."

"He's young and eager . . ."

"Yes, and he can be dangerous if he isn't stopped. He'll have the whole town in a state of chaos, and I don't think I have to tell you where that could lead. Fear breeds fear, and makes people do crazy things. Perhaps he'll listen to you. After all, you're running for mayor next year, and that has to count for something."

Elmer Dodd stood up. "I'll do what I can, but

I can't make any promises. The kid has a mind of his own, just like his daddy.''

He had reached the door when Jennifer said, ''Oh, by the way, if you see Dan Wise, tell him I've been trying to reach him. His dog can go home tomorrow.''

Elmer put his hat on his head and frowned. ''I saw him this morning, but he didn't say anything about his dog.''

''The dog had a bone stuck in its trachea, and it had to be surgically removed.''

Elmer Dodd nodded, and left the clinic, but not before Jennifer caught the expression on his face. All the way home, she tried to identify it, but it wasn't until she'd pulled in behind the church and parked the Jeep in her slot that she realized that it was something close to fear. There was no other way to describe it.

Surprised to find Willy in the kitchen with Emma and her grandfather, Jennifer gave hugs around, before she said, ''I don't like the looks on your faces. I have the feeling Ben and I aren't the only ones who have had a difficult day.''

''Difficult doesn't quite cover it,'' Willy said, running a hand through his dark, tousled hair. ''I was besieged from the moment I unlocked my office door, and it went on all day. Even followed me into court. Finally, the judge had to clear the courtroom because of the hecklers in the gallery. And the questions were all the same, and they were all preceded with, 'Do we have a killer running around the streets of Calico?' Wexler's story in the morning paper sure stirred things up. I tried calling the clinic, but got the switchboard. Said you were only taking emergency calls, and I can understand that.''

"Same kind of upheaval here," Wes said wearily. "Finally had to take the phone off the hook."

Emma was cutting up a chicken, and stabbed at a wing. "Had to quit answering the door, too. It's pure craziness, Jennifer. I'm glad you got home safe and sound."

"Amen," Wes said. "Willy is staying for dinner, sweetheart. We decided it's about time we talk this out. The sheriff is coming, too, because we need his input. I think we all expected a few repercussions after that story in the paper, but from what I saw and heard today, I have the feeling it's already gone too far. People are scared, and God only knows what they'll do. I'd hate to think of the town full up with vigilantes wearing guns on their hips, but it sure is a possibility."

Emma muttered, "Wouldn't that be something!"

Jennifer sighed. "I have a lot to tell you, but I'll wait for the sheriff. Do I have time to freshen up?"

Wes nodded. "The sheriff should be here any minute, but dinner is a long way off."

Emma gave a *hr-rump*. "Because I forgot to get the chicken out of the freezer, and had to defrost it under running water. And don't you say one word about defrosting it in the microwave, because that clean slipped my mind too."

Feeling terrible because everyone had had to endure so much, Jennifer went up to her room with heavy steps. She wanted to make things better, but how could she when in her heart she knew they were only going to get worse.

Twenty minutes later, wearing clean jeans and a pink cotton blouse, Jennifer joined the glum group in the kitchen, who were sitting around the table drinking coffee. The sheriff had arrived, and Jennifer's heart twisted at the sight of his weary face. "Let me guess," she said. "You've had to deal with a three-ring circus all day."

"Yeah, and Elmer Dodd. Finally had to block off the road near the dumps, and call in two more deputies. It's gotten out of hand, and I don't know what to do about it."

Jennifer poured a cup of coffee, and sat down

beside Willy. "Elmer Dodd stopped by the clinic this afternoon, and we had a talk. . . ."

"Harassing you, too, huh?" the sheriff said.

"Actually, he was rather congenial, which was certainly a surprise. He wanted some answers, said you were giving him the brush-off, and I tried my best to assure him the only reason you've cordoned off the area is because of all the sinkholes, not because those boys found a bone. I also told him he should talk to John, Jr., because if he keeps printing stories like the one in the paper this morning, it's going to do more harm than good."

"And what did he say to that?" Wes asked.

"Said he'd try, but couldn't make any promises. Said that John, Jr., had a mind of his own, like his daddy."

"Pick up your coffee cups," Emma said, shaking out a flowered tablecloth. "We're going to eat right here instead of in the dining room, because I don't want to be running back and forth. I don't want to miss one word!"

The sheriff managed a wan smile. "Don't mind eating in the kitchen, Emma. And the chicken smells great. My wife is feeling a might under the weather, so I'd have to nuke a TV dinner."

Emma managed a smile, too. "It's called Heewaiian chicken. Fancy name for chicken and pineapple. Low-fat, low-calorie, just the way Jennifer likes it.''

The sheriff's expression was strained, and Jennifer frowned. "Oh-oh, you don't like pineapple."

"No, it's not that . . . It's just . . . Well, it's been a rough day, and I'm just trying to unwind, that's all. So what else did Dodd say?"

"Not much, actually. But there was one curious thing. He was about to leave when I mentioned Dan Wise and the dog. I told him I'd been trying to reach Mr. Wise all day regarding Einstein's release. He said he'd seen Dan Wise earlier, but that he hadn't mentioned the dog. I told him about the dog getting a bone stuck in its trachea, and the emergency surgery. No big deal in itself, if it hadn't been for the strange look on his face. Took me a while to figure it out, but I finally came to the conclusion it was fear, or maybe anxiety."

"Maybe he's afraid the dog found the bone on his property, and Dan Wise might sue him," Willy said.

"The dog *did* find the bone on his property," the sheriff replied.

"I'm talking about the dairy. Think about it. The dog is running around the dairy, finds a bone, swallows it, nearly dies, and the owner sues. Dodd just went through a mess with the senior citizens, so why not? Everybody is sue happy these days. Anything for a buck.''

"The prospect of another lawsuit might make him angry," Jennifer reasoned, ''but I don't think it would fill him full of fear, or even anxiety. I've decided it must be something else.''

Emma was chopping vegetables for a salad, absently making mush of the tomatoes. Finally, she turned around and waved the knife. *The Bone Yard* by Michael Tarcher. It's sitting right on the library shelf. One of those mystery books Jennifer has been collecting over the years. A man kills his wife and buries her body in the backyard. Eight years later, while he's away on vacation, an underground waterpipe breaks, and the daughter calls the plumber. They dig up the backyard, and find the bones. What if Elmer Dodd killed Bernice and the traveling salesman, and buried their bodies on that piece of land?''

Jennifer's heart was thumping in her chest as she responded. ''It occurred to us that Elmer Dodd bought that plot of land because he had plans to expand the dairy. But he never did. Why?''

"*Hr-rump*. Because before he could get to it, he killed those two and buried them. Couldn't expand then. Couldn't chance uncovering the bodies.

I always said it was strange the way that woman left. Supposedly took off with that traveling salesman, but nobody actually saw the traveling salesman. Just had Elmer's word for it. And everybody in town who was around then knows what a volatile marriage that was. I remember one time they were in the Mercantile arguing. They were shoving each other around, and everybody heard Bernice tell him how she was going to kill him some night in his bed, and put an end to their miserable marriage. Well, maybe he beat her to it.''

All eyes were on Emma, staring at her in amazement. She flushed, and went back to the salad, but not before saying, "Well, it could've happened that way. The skeletons *were* found on his property, and he *is* an evil man."

Jennifer took a deep, ragged breath. "And maybe, just maybe, that's why Elmer Dodd looked so frightened when I mentioned the dog and the bone. Was he wondering if the dog had found a part of the skeleton on the property? Put that together with the bone the kids found, and it would be enough to throw him into a panic. And maybe that's why he tried to be nice to me today when he stopped by the clinic. He wanted answers, and knew he wouldn't get anywhere with me if he was hostile and abrasive."

The sheriff loosened his tie, like he couldn't get enough air. And now, all eyes were on him. He finally shrugged. "Well, I guess it could've happened that way, but I think it's really reaching. Guess we'll just have to wait for the report from Washington. . . . Well, nuts. This isn't the time or place for this, what with dinner cooking on the stove, but . . . Well, I was going to wait until after dinner to tell you. . . . Well, nuts. I . . . We found a gun."

Everybody gasped in unison, and the sheriff went on. "Little pearl-handled twenty-two-caliber. Not much of a weapon from a distance, but it can sure mess things up at close range. The bullets don't go through. Just sort of spin around inside a body and turn everything to mush. No latents, so I figure it's either been in the ground too long, or was wiped clean."

Jennifer was the first to speak. "Do you think those two people were shot, and the gun was the murder weapon?"

"Looks like. Ah . . . well, we also found the skulls . . ."

Wes choked on a swallow of coffee, and Jennifer and Emma gasped again.

Willy coughed, and cleared his throat. "Where?"

"Same spot, only higher up. Maybe a foot apart. When the sinkhole opened up and the skeletons took a tumble, the skulls, being round and full of rifts, got caught in a tangle of dead roots, and didn't drop all the way down."

"And you shipped them off to Washington?" Jennifer asked.

"No, not yet. It was late this afternoon when we found them. Not enough time to get them boxed and all the paperwork done before the post office closed."

Jennifer was afraid to ask. "So where *are* they?"

"In the trunk of my car."

Willy spouted, "Holy moly!"

"Yeah, well there's more. We found a bullet lodged in the back part of one of the skulls. Small caliber, but it did the job. You can see where it smushed up the forehead going through. More than likely, the twenty-two."

Silence followed his announcement.

"Any way to tell how old the bullet is?" Willy asked finally, a little raggedly, like he, too, was trying to suck in air.

"Not really, but I can tell you right now it isn't part of Calico's past. My guess, it's a modern-day bullet, we've got a bona fide double murder on our hands, and the nightmare is just beginning.''

Emma clucked her tongue. ''Modern-day, but like maybe fifteen or sixteen years ago? It's been about that long since Bernice supposedly took off with the salesman.''

''Maybe.''

Jennifer was shaking her head. ''You can't leave the skulls in the trunk of your car, Sheriff. What if your car is stolen, or gets broken into?''

Wes swallowed the rest of his coffee in one gulp, and wiped his mouth on a flowered napkin. ''Jennifer is right, Sheriff. We all hate to think about things like that happening in Calico, but we all know they can, even in a church parking lot. Best you bring them in the house. You can put them in my study until after dinner. . . .''

Emma said excitedly, ''Nobody has much of an appetite now, Mr. Wes, and dinner will keep. Oh! My heart is jumping clean up in my throat!''

Jennifer wasn't sure what she felt, but welcomed Willy's strong arm around her shoulder, as they made their way into the study.

A few minutes later, the sheriff carried the box into the room, removed the plastic-wrapped skulls, and carefully placed them on the desk. Everybody held their breaths while he unwrapped them, and then they could only stare. Several smaller bones around the cheek area in one of the skulls were missing but, for the most part, it was intact, including the teeth. It was also the skull with the bullet. The severe damage to the forehead was clearly evident. The larger skull was in worse shape, but still had a few teeth.

The sheriff had adjusted the green lampshade for better light, and Jennifer looked around the warm, cozy room she had always loved so much, and tried to focus her attention on the dark-wood paneling and book-lined shelves, her grandfather's brown-leather reading chair—anything to bring some normalcy to the insane picture the leering skulls were creating. The eyes were gone, of course, but the open, gaping sockets made it even worse.

"Maybe you should try and get Bernice Dodd's dental records to send off with the skulls," Willy said, moving around the desk to examine the skulls from all angles. "And take a look at the comparison in size. I'd say one is a man, and one is a woman."

"Then you really think there's a chance we're looking at Bernice Dodd and the traveling salesman?" Wes asked, leaning down closer to the skulls.

"Yes, I do," Willy said, "because it all fits. And it makes a lot more sense than having two bodies turn up when nobody in town has been reported missing."

The sheriff ran a hand through his thinning hair. "Asking for Bernice Dodd's dental records could cause added problems. Portias Landers was the only dentist in town back then, and likes to gossip almost as much as Cottie Anderson. What do you suppose he'll think if I ask him for Bernice Dodd's dental records? I guarantee he'll put two and two together, and he won't keep quiet about it."

"Not even if you tell him to?" Willy asked.

"That would probably make it worse, because then he'd know for sure something sinister was afoot. All he'd have to do is spill it to one person, and within a couple of hours, everybody in town would know. And it wouldn't take them long to put two and two together, either. Might even scare Dodd off, and we sure don't want that to happen, if, in fact, Dodd is the killer. I think the best thing to do is ship the skulls off tomorrow as planned, wait for the results, and go from there. If the Feds tell us the victims are a male and female around the right ages, and that they've been dead around fifteen or sixteen years, I'll have enough to subpoena the dental records, and bring Dodd in for questioning. And the element of surprise would be in our favor.''

"And then we'd have to prove Elmer Dodd killed them," Willy said thoughtfully. "I can see him playing innocent, and claiming the traveling salesman must have killed her, and then he killed himself."

Wes said, "Maybe that's exactly what happened."

Jennifer shook her head. "If it happened that way, who buried the bodies?"

Emma let out a hoot. "That's the way to think, Jennifer. Just like *Matlock* on TV. That man gets his teeth into a case, and he never turns loose until it's solved. Speaking of teeth. Got me a filling about ready to pop out. Been chewing on one side of my mouth for days. Maybe it's time I go see old Portias. Don't need an appointment these days. Most of the folks go to that new dental office near the hospital. Bet I could get in to see old Portias first thing in the morning. Maybe even before you get the skulls boxed up, Sheriff. Would sure hurry things along if you could include the dental records. Nothing lost if one of 'em isn't Bernice, but what if it is?"

The sheriff eyed Emma intently. "You think you could do that without causing suspicion?"

Emma beamed. "Watch me. I wouldn't tape down the box until you hear from me, that's for sure."

Jennifer curled up in her grandfather's reading chair, trying to channel all the questions that were running around in her head. "I never really knew Bernice Dodd, but I vaguely remember a brother?"

The sheriff said, "You're thinking about Dodd's older brother, Roland, who owns a meat packaging plant in Omaha, Jennifer. He's the one whose son is a vet. Anyway, the Dodd family saga covers a lot of years, but it isn't complicated. Elmer's mother died when he was in high school, and the father died when he was in his late twenties. He was running the dairy then, and knew all the ins and outs. The dairy was left to both brothers, but Roland didn't want any part of it. Elmer met Bernice while he was visiting his brother in Omaha, and they were married a month later. She'd never been married, and she was a hairdresser. No story there. He brought her back to Calico, and built her that big house across the river. She settled in just fine as Dodd's wife, and opened up a beauty shop. I know for a fact they fought about that. He wanted her to stay home.''

''Apparently they fought about a lot of things,'' Jennifer said. ''Makes you wonder what went on behind closed doors.''

''Makes you wonder,'' Wes repeated. ''I never could get them to come to church. Bernice was a strange lady. She liked the idea of being Elmer's wife, she was supposedly a good hairdresser, but she was never a part of Calico. Never could get close to anybody. Had an 'uppity' way about her that turned people off.''

''Like Elmer Dodd,'' the sheriff said. ''They made a good pair.''

Jennifer said, ''Cottie Anderson liked her. Or at least she liked the way Bernice fixed her hair.''

Emma muttered, ''Hmmm, and now there she is, with her head a-sitting on Mr. Wes's desk. Gives me the chills, that's for sure.''

The sheriff wrapped the skulls and returned them to the box before he said, ''We're assuming one of the skulls is Bernice, when we haven't any proof. Let's not jump to conclusions until all the facts are in.''

''And the dental records?'' Emma asked. ''You still want me to get 'em?''

The sheriff sighed. ''I didn't ask you to get

them, Emma. That was your idea, but I won't try and stop you.''

Emma smiled. ''What you're saying is, you'll look the other way. That's fine with me. Now, let's go in the kitchen and eat. I said the chicken would keep. I didn't say it would keep forever.''

It was after midnight when Jennifer went downstairs for a glass of milk, and found her grandfather sitting at the kitchen table with a plate of brownies in front of him. He was in his pajamas and wearing his comfortable terry robe, but sleep seemed to be the furthest thing from his mind.

He gave her a sheepish grin, and shrugged. ''What can I say? Emma made the brownies this morning, right in the middle of all that chaos. It was her way of rebelling, I guess. Or maybe it was simply a matter of trying to bring some normalcy into the day.''

Jennifer kissed his cheek. ''A brownie and a glass of milk sounds wonderful, Grandfather. I'd like to have things back to normal, too, but I don't see how that's going to happen. At least not until Elmer Dodd is behind bars.''

Wes waited until Jennifer had the milk poured and a brownie in her hand before he said, ''Then you really think Elmer Dodd is the killer?''

"Yes, I do, but I also know proving it isn't going to be easy."

He watched her bite into the brownie, and with a twinkle in his blue eyes, said, "Think a special prayer or two might help?"

"I think it would help a lot," she said, giving him a dimpled grin. "And while you're at it, tell God I'm going to work out twice as hard tomorrow, and might even jog to the river. My penitence for eating this scrumptious brownie."

Wes squeezed her hand, and bowed his head.

Chapter Six

Disheartened, because it had been over a week and they still hadn't heard from the F.B.I., Jennifer had taken the afternoon off, and had ridden Tassie to her special spot overlooking the valley. She hadn't bothered with lunch, but had brought along a packet of trail mix, and sat munching on it now, amid the carpet of orange and yellow wildflowers that covered the small rise.

Tassie nickered softly, and swished her tail. Jennifer smiled. "I know, lovely lady. I've missed this spot too, but so much has been going on. Well, I guess that's a lie. *Nothing* has been going on, and that's the problem."

Jennifer breathed in deeply of the warm after-

noon air, feeling and seeing a touch of fall everywhere. Cornfields had been plowed under, and off
in the distance, the lion-colored grasses had taken
on a russet hue. Even the sky was a lighter blue,
and the sun a pale yellow. It was almost Labor
Day, and the town was already preparing for the
big three-day weekend. The citizens, though still
mindful of all that had happened, were calmer
now, thanks to John, Jr.'s, follow-up story in *The
Calico Review*, wherein he had admitted to over-
reacting, and that the sheriff had every right to
protect the town from a dangerous plot of land
any way he deemed necessary. And if that meant
cordoning it off, so be it. He hadn't mentioned the
bone the boys had found, and had concluded by
saying the owner was making arrangements to fill
in the sinkholes and fence the property. He had
stopped short of actually apologizing, but had alluded to the fact that everybody makes mistakes.
It was also clear Elmer Dodd had talked to him,
and had gotten the point across, which meant she,
in turn, had gotten to Elmer Dodd, and for that
she could only feel a great deal of satisfaction.

But oh, if John, Jr., Dodd, and the town only
knew what was going on behind the scenes!
Emma, who had a wonderfully creative mind, had
gotten Nettie Balkin to help her get Bernice

Dodd's dental records, and the plan had been a complete success. While Emma was in the dentist chair, complaining about her loose filling, Nettie had barged into the outer office, and had confronted the dental assistant/receptionist, claiming Portias had overcharged her for the gold crown he had put in a few weeks before. Portias had gone into the outer office to try and calm Nettie down, leaving Emma free to go into the little side room where the outdated records were kept. Within minutes, Emma had the file tucked under her full skirt, held in place by a firm hand, and had scooted out, claiming she had to get home because she'd forgotten to turn off the teakettle. She had left Nettie arguing with Portias, and had hurried to the sheriff's office, waving the file and exclaiming triumphantly, "You didn't tape down the top of the box, did you?" It had been an exhilarating, exciting moment, made even better when Nettie arrived a short time later, giggling her head off. The sheriff kept saying, "I don't want to know how you two did it," but there was excitement dancing in his eyes, too, as he placed the file in the box with the skulls, and taped down the top.

But now the excitement they'd all felt that day had turned to apprehension. Because in this case, no news *wasn't* good news. If one of the skeletons wasn't Bernice Dodd, they were no closer to solving the mystery than before.

Jennifer heard a horse whinny on the trail, and turned. It was Willy astride a chestnut gelding, and the sight of him warmed her heart. He was wearing jeans, boots, and a University of Nebraska "Cornhusker" sweatshirt, but it wasn't until she saw the expression on his face that she realized something big had happened. He was grinning from ear to ear, for one thing, and his cheeks looked flushed with excitement.

Jennifer's heart pounded in her chest, as she said, "I'll bet the sheriff heard from the F.B.I."

Willy tethered the gelding to a tree, and joined her on the little rise before he said, "He sure did, and even better than that, one skeleton was a male, and the other skeleton was Bernice Dodd. No bullet in the male, but they found the point of entry."

Speechless, and a little breathless, Jennifer threw her arms around Willy.

He held her tenderly, and murmured, "I know. Makes you think we must be doing something right."

Jennifer shook her head in awe, not quite grasping the significance of what he had told her. "How did you know where to find me?"

"I talked to Ben. He said you were taking Tassie for a ride. I went to the stable, rented the fastest horse Max has, and figured this was where you'd be. When you were a kid, even before your grandfather gave you Tassie for a birthday present, this was your special place when you had a lot on your mind. I remember the day you brought me out here, and told me *I* was special, and that was why you wanted to share it with me.''

Jennifer leaned her head against his shoulder. ''You are special, Willy. More than you'll ever know. Thanks for bringing me the good news. Or is it good news? I mean we still have to prove Elmer Dodd is the killer, so it isn't over. Maybe the real nightmare is just beginning.''

''I know. The sheriff all but said the same thing. When I left him, he was on his way to talk to Judge Stoker. He needs a search warrant, and plans on bringing Dodd in for questioning.''

Jennifer shook her head. ''Search warrant? I don't understand.''

''Unless Dodd confesses, or some other incriminating evidence pops up, there won't be enough for an indictment, Jenny. The sheriff is hoping to find the evidence. Some shred of something— anything—to connect him to the murders. Otherwise, Dodd is going to walk.''

''He can't get off, Willy. He just *can't!*''

"Innocent until proven guilty," Willy reminded her.

"I know, but he's guilty. I can *feel* it."

Willy looked at his watch. "Shall we start back? The sheriff said we can sit in on the interrogation. He thinks you intimidate the man, and that might help."

Jennifer mounted Tassie, and shook her head. "I don't think I intimidate him at all, and he isn't going to say 'boo' without having an attorney present."

"I'm an attorney."

Jennifer's mouth dropped open. "You're not thinking of defending him, are you? I mean, if it goes that far."

Willy grinned. "Wouldn't dream of it, but that doesn't mean I can't watch out for his rights during the interrogation, to speed things along. What happens after that is his problem. Knowing him, he'll bring somebody in. Some hotshot attorney from Omaha, maybe even New York. All of this is conjecture, of course, because if the sheriff doesn't find the evidence he needs, the whole thing is moot anyway."

Jennifer urged Tassie down the trail, and felt a deep sense of foreboding. They were so close, and yet so far, and they weren't talking about some derelict or transient passing through town. They were talking about Elmer Dodd, self-proclaimed upstanding citizen, who planned to run for mayor! And the thought of that happening chilled her to the bone.

Because they'd had to take the horses back to the stable and pick up their vehicles, it was a good hour later before Jennifer and Willy walked into the sheriff's office. They found Nettie alone, chewing on her nails, and pacing the floor.

"I'm sure glad to see you," she said, waving a hand at the coffeepot. "Help yourself. I've had enough to float a fleet of ships. I expected the sheriff back before this, and all I can do is wonder. Maybe he couldn't find Dodd."

"What about the search warrant?" Willy asked, pouring coffee into two Styrofoam cups.

"The judge signed the search warrant, and said to keep him posted. Said he knew all along that someday, Dodd was going to take a bad fall. That's off the record, of course. The deputies are doing the searching. At Dodd's house, and at the dairy. Guess you know they had better find something, because that man will never confess."

Jennifer sat down on the little bench near the window, and took a sip of coffee before she said,

"When I was driving over from the stable, I looked at all the red, white and blue banners and flags, and all I could think about is how this is going to affect the Labor Day festivities. The town is finally settling down, and now this."

Nettie shrugged. "A tornado could whip through, and we'd still celebrate Labor Day. Holidays mean a lot to the folks in Calico. About all I see happening is that the town will take sides, whether we can prove Dodd killed his wife or not. Some will think he's guilty, no matter what, and some will think he's innocent, no matter what. How he handles that is his problem. But I know one thing for sure. He'd better reconsider running for mayor, because if there is even one shred of doubt, he won't get the votes."

"You make it sound as though he's going to get off, Nettie."

She raised a brow. "And you don't think he will? Look at the facts, Jennifer. Two skeletons were found on Dodd's property, along with a gun. One of 'em was his wife, and the other one was probably the traveling salesman. That's it. What we need is proof Dodd pulled the trigger, and personally, I don't think that's going to happen. I think he's going to come up with a story like you've never heard before. I know that man too well. He's a good con artist, and he has a way of twisting things around to suit his purpose. And as far as finding incriminating evidence, no way. Not after sixteen years.''

"Then what are they looking for?" Jennifer asked. "I mean, are they looking for something specific?"

"Ammunition that matches the murder weapon, a diary, notes, personal letters, that sort of thing, but I'll tell you right now, it's a waste of time."

"I can't see him keeping stuff like that around, either," Jennifer reasoned, "but even if he did, what if it's locked away in a safe?"

"Dodd doesn't have a safe, and as far as I know, never did. He's like his daddy was, afraid he'll forget the combination, or the lock will get jammed. He doesn't trust banks, either, although he has two accounts at the bank. One business, one personal, but no safe deposit box. Rumor is, he keeps most of his money in a mattress. Real dumb, but he's not dumb enough to keep incriminating evidence lying around. Mark my words, he'll be out on the street in a few hours, and it'll be business as usual."

"Try and think positive," Willy said. "If he killed once, he can kill again, and nobody wants to have to share the sidewalk with a murderer."

Jennifer shuddered, and was about to say they'd been sharing the sidewalk with a murderer for sixteen years, when the sheriff and Elmer Dodd walked in. Dodd was wearing brown slacks and a white shirt, and was carrying his tie. He wasn't cuffed, but he still had the look of a man who was being restrained. Wild, darting eyes, full of the same kind of fear Jennifer had seen that day in the clinic.

He glanced around the room, and his eyes settled on Willy first. "Trying to drum up business, counselor?" he said with a smirk, though his voice cracked. And then he looked at Jennifer. "And is there a reason why *you're* here?"

"I was invited," Jennifer said, lifting her chin a notch.

"Sit down," the sheriff ordered, in a no-nonsense tone. "I don't plan on being here all night."

Dodd sat down in a chair near the desk, and drummed his beefy fingers along the edge. And again, his words were directed at Willy. "You might as well go home, counselor. I already told the sheriff I don't need no lawyer. I didn't kill my wife, and I didn't kill the traveling salesman!" He looked up at the ceiling, and tears filled his eyes.

"I should've known something was going to happen when that man showed me that gun."

The sheriff spread out several sheets of paper on his desk, and opened a notebook. "You wouldn't say much of anything on the way into town, Dodd, and now you're jumping ahead, and getting everybody confused. Why don't you just let me ask the questions? We'll start from the beginning, and take it nice and easy, so we can get it all down." He spoke into a small tape recorder, giving the date and time and who was in the room, making sure it was clear there was an attorney present, no matter whether Elmer wanted one or not.

"Okay. State your name for the record."

Dodd rolled his eyes, but said, "Elmer Edward Dodd."

His date of birth and address came next.

"Uh-huh. Okay. Can you remember the exact date your wife disappeared? The date you thought she left with the traveling salesman?"

"No, but it was around the middle of June. I was in Omaha when she took off. . . . God, this is so hard. . . . Got back, and she was gone, along with two suitcases and some of her clothes."

"Only some of her clothes?"

"Yeah. The good stuff. Stuff I bought her after we were married."

"And the salesman's name?"

Elmer Dodd scratched his head. "Think it was Davidson, or something like that. He was selling encyclopedias, and was on his way to Sioux Falls. Bernice met him in the Mercantile. She was buying material to make kitchen curtains, and he was buying a map of Nebraska, or so she said."

"Did you know she was planning to run away with him?"

"No, I didn't. I knew she was sweet on him, but I didn't think too much about it. She liked to flirt. No big deal."

"How long was he in town?"

"Maybe a week. If I'd known what was happening between them and what they were planning, I wouldn't have gone to Omaha."

"Where was he staying?"

"In the two-bedroom cottage at the dairy. I know what that sounds like. Like I was a real buffoon, but see, Bernice brought him home, fed him a meal, and said he needed a place to stay. Dumb me didn't see the sparks flying between them, and when he gave me five hundred dollars for a week, I didn't see the harm. Money was money, and I had the empty cottage. You know,

I haven't been able to rent that cottage out since. I use it for storage.'' He looked at the ceiling again, and this time, tears ran down his cheeks.

"Are the cottages numbered?" The sheriff asked.

Elmer Dodd nodded. "That one is 3-A."

The sheriff spoke to Nettie. "Get on the radio and tell the boys to search cottage 3-A at the dairy." He smiled at Elmer. "Guess I don't have to tell you. I got a search warrant. Okay, so you came home from Omaha and she was gone. Did the salesman have a car?"

"Yeah. A dark green sedan."

"Why did you think she'd run off with the salesman?"

"What would *you* think? He was gone, she was gone, and her clothes were gone."

"Then she didn't leave you a note?"

"No. Now I know why. She didn't run off with him at all. He took her out to that desolate plot of land, and killed her. . . ." Deep breath. "I'll bet he had it figured out where he'd bury the body all along. I kept waiting for her to come back, but she didn't." His voice quavered. "And to think she was right out there on my property, dead and buried."

"Then who killed the salesman?" the sheriff asked.

Dodd shrugged. "Maybe he killed himself."

Jennifer spoke up. "Then who buried the bodies?"

He looked at her and scowled. "How in hell should I know?"

The sheriff went on. "You mentioned a gun?"

"Yeah. The guy cleaned his gun that night Bernice invited him to dinner. Said it wasn't safe traveling around the country without it."

"Do you remember what kind of gun it was?"

"No . . . A gun is a gun. I was nervous the whole time. Always been afraid of guns. I have my daddy's gun collection, but it's locked up behind glass. Someday I'll sell it, if I can find the right buyer." He took another deep breath. "Guess I should thank Donald Attwater for selling me that plot of land, instead of cursing him. See, he knew it wasn't worth a pile of beans, but convinced me it was. Talked about how great it would be if I could expand the dairy, and blew smoke right through my ears. Later, when I found out the truth, I confronted him and told him before I was through God and everybody was gonna know what a shyster he was. He offered to buy it back, but I had a better idea."

"Like telling him you wanted the mayor's job?" the sheriff asked.

"Yeah. He's been the mayor for years because nobody else wanted the job. Just sitting there, collecting his salary. He planned dying in the mayor's chair. Well, I told him all that was gonna change. That someday, he was gonna step down, and I was gonna be the mayor. I never had any intentions of running for mayor in the beginning. It was just something I enjoyed holding over his head. But then about a year ago, I got to thinking about it, and decided it might be a smart move. The funny thing is, through it all, we've gotten to be pretty good friends. We think alike, and we understand each other, and that's what's gonna make this whole thing so easy. He steps down, and I move in."

"What if somebody else decides to run for mayor too?" Willy asked.

Elmer scowled. "Nobody wanted the job back then, and nobody wants it now." He shook his head, as though he suddenly remembered why he was in the sheriff's office. "Ah, like I was saying, I guess I should thank him. If that sinkhole hadn't opened up . . ." He ran his fingers over his eyes. "I guess that . . . I guess those boys who found the bone . . . Guess it was a part of my wife, or

. . . I know you did right, Sheriff. You couldn't tell anybody, not even me. You said you sent my wife's . . . my wife's bones to Washington, D.C., for identification, but you didn't say what they were going to do with them. I mean, I'd like to give her a proper burial. . . .''

The sheriff cleared his throat. ''The Feds are sending your wife's remains back to us, Dodd, but they are keeping the unidentified man. Now about the gun . . .''

Jennifer listened to the exchange between the two men, and decided Elmer Dodd really was incredible. He had twisted things around, just like Nettie said he would, and he had come up with a story ''like she had never heard before.'' He was good. He was very, very good, and their chances of getting him were slipping further and further away. He knew the sheriff wouldn't find any incriminating evidence, and this was all a game. And he was playing it to win.

Elmer was saying, ''Do I have the right to know where your boys are looking, and what they're looking for?''

''No harm in that, because you're staying put until I get word from my men, one way or the other. They're searching your house, garage, and your office at the dairy, and you heard my orders to search the cottage. And they're looking for anything that might connect you to the murders. That's all I can tell you at this time. I've given my men instructions to be neat, but you know how that goes.''

Dodd nodded. ''Of course I do, and I understand. They're just doing their job, and you're just doing yours.''

The sheriff scribbled in his notebook. ''Can you give me a description of the traveling salesman?''

''Dark, thin, maybe forty. That would make him about fifty-six now. Think his first name was Al, or Alfred, or Alcot. Something like that. You know, my brother told me Bernice was going to be trouble when I married her. He said she had a 'flirting' eye. Should've listened to him. Maybe she'd still be alive.'' Big sigh. ''But I loved her. God, how I loved her.''

Jennifer looked at Willy, but couldn't tell what he was thinking. But he was very attentive, and took in every word. Was he thinking the man might be telling the truth? He told a convincing story, and Willy was an attorney, which meant innocent until proven guilty. Unfortunately, she didn't think it was going to go that far.

Jennifer's fears were substantiated later, when the deputies wearily walked into the office. The sheriff had asked Elmer Dodd the same questions, over and over again, and there hadn't been any variance, and everybody was weary.

"We didn't find squat," Manny Pressman said. "And we looked everywhere. We found a gun collection in the house. Army issue stuff from long ago, couple of target pistols—wrong caliber, and a thirty-thirty Winchester deer rifle. Found some ammunition too, but nothing to match up with the murder weapon."

The sheriff sighed. "Well, I guess that's it. You're free to go, Dodd, but I wouldn't leave town. We might need to question you again."

Elmer Dodd stood up, and shook the sheriff's hand. "Don't worry, Sheriff. I have no intentions of leaving town. This is my home, and I want my name cleared. Oh, and don't worry about John, Jr., over at *The Calico Review*. I'll talk to him, and make sure he prints an accurate accounting. The last thing we need is to have all the town folks stirred up again just before Labor Day. Guess I forgot to tell you. I'm the grand marshal in the parade this year. Thought it was a good idea, what with me running for mayor and all. . . ." Tears filled his eyes. "I was looking forward to it, but now . . ." He shook his head, and walked out.

One of the deputies took Elmer Dodd home, leaving the group in the sheriff's office to ponder and fret. But the sheriff said it best. "That man is a miserable example of a human being. He knows he's got us, and was playing the scene for all it was worth. Unfortunately, my hands are tied. Jennifer?"

Jennifer was standing at the window, looking through the blinds at the darkening shadows. Streetlights had popped on, and the street was nearly void of traffic. Everybody was heading home, to share dinner with their families. She turned and looked at the sheriff. "Something isn't sitting well, Sheriff Cody. I have this 'feeling,' but it's just out of reach. I know you understand what I'm talking about. It's that elusive something I can't put my finger on."

"Oh-oh," Willy said. "Here we go again."

The sheriff, who knew Jennifer well enough to know her feelings shouldn't be taken lightly, said, "Would it help if I played back the tape?"

"Maybe. It couldn't hurt."

For the next hour or so, Elmer Dodd's voice filled the room, and when the tape finally wound down, Jennifer was left with two thoughts. First, the man had been totally convincing. She put the other thought into a question. "If Elmer Dodd killed his wife and the salesman, what did he do with the salesman's car? If Bernice was planning to run off with the salesman, the car was probably loaded down with their things. I don't imagine Dodd had much trouble getting rid of it all. He could have buried it or burned it. But what about the car?''

The sheriff scratched his chin. ''Probably drove it to Omaha, stripped it, and ditched it. Probably rode the bus back to Calico, or maybe his brother brought him home.''

Jennifer sighed. ''I can't help it, Sheriff. I still have the feeling we're missing something.''

The sheriff said, ''Well, when you remember what it is, call me. I don't care what time it is. I don't care if it's in the middle of the night.

''Now, I don't know about anybody else, but I'm going home. This has been one awful day, and my head feels like I got it caught in a vise.''

Jennifer had a headache too, and felt a deep sense of dread. Maybe Elmer Dodd wasn't the killer. But if he wasn't, who was?

Chapter Seven

Jennifer overslept the following morning, after spending hours the night before discussing all that had happened with her grandfather and Emma. In a flurry, she showered, dressed, and headed for the kitchen to grab a quick cup of coffee, and was met by Emma's smiling face. "You can relax, young lady. Ben called. Because of the holiday weekend, the clinic is closed until Tuesday morning, except for emergencies."

Jennifer sighed, and dropped to a chair. "I talked to him last night, and he didn't say anything about it."

"Because he made the decision this morning. Said you both deserved a little time off, though I would suspect Irene had something to do with it.

She's in charge of the senior citizens' float in the parade, so probably needs his strong arms.''

Suddenly confronted with four days off, Jennifer shook her head. "What am I going to do with myself for four whole days, Emma? This is the first Labor Day weekend I've been home in six years, and it just sort of crept up on me. And everybody seems to have everything under control."

"You just relax and enjoy it, my dear, and you can begin by meeting Willy for lunch. He called earlier, and wants you to meet him in Calico Park at noon. No ifs, ands or buts."

Jennifer nodded at the jars of strawberry jam lined up on the counter, shimmering like red jewels in the mid-morning sunlight. "And I suppose you've been up since dawn, putting up jam?"

Emma gave one of the jars a loving pat. "That I have. I'm entering the jam contest at the Grange on Sunday. Entering the apple pie contest, too, and might even try my hand at the chili cook-off, if I have the time."

"And Grandfather?"

"He left bright and early for a breakfast meeting. He's on the committee for the big barbecue on Monday."

Jennifer's mouth turned down. "I feel terrible,

Emma. I kept the two of you up all hours last night, talking about Elmer Dodd and what's going on in my life, when there is so much going on in yours. Why didn't you say something?''

''Because what you had to say was important, Jennifer, much more important than the Labor Day festivities. But I'd like to see a smile on your face, so I'll give you a little advice. Let it go for the next few days. Elmer Dodd isn't going anywhere, and there isn't anything you can do anyway. By the way, didn't you say he was going to give John, Jr., over at *The Calico Review* an 'accurate accounting'?''

''That's what he said.''

''*Hr-rump*. Well, read it for yourself, but I'd say he left a few things out.''

Jennifer picked up the paper, and gritted her teeth. She hadn't expected Elmer to give John, Jr., an accurate accounting, but she had expected John, Jr., to run with whatever Elmer gave him, and print a two-page dramatic narrative. But as she scanned the article, she was surprised to see that it was a very brief sketch at best. Simply put, the sheriff had discovered human bones on Elmer Dodd's land south of town, and Dodd was calling for the citizens to give the sheriff their complete cooperation while the matter was under investigation.

Jennifer tossed the paper aside, and muttered, "It's accurate enough, but like you said, it just isn't complete."

"Sounds to me like Elmer Dodd was just trying to save his skin. So maybe the sheriff should have a little talk with Mr. John Wexler, Jr., and tell him what's *really* going on."

"But that's just it, Emma, there isn't a darned thing going on except a lot of speculation. The sheriff still has to prove Elmer Dodd is the killer, or like Willy says, the whole thing is moot."

"Moot?" Emma scoffed. "What kind of a word is that?"

"It means insignificant, irrelevant, meaningless. And even if John, Jr., had printed the facts, it wouldn't prove anything."

"Ah, but it would cast a shadow of suspicion on that man. Think about it. Two skeletons found buried on Dodd's property. One of them was Dodd's wife. Sixteen years ago, she supposedly ran off with a traveling salesman. Doesn't that say it all?"

Jennifer sighed. "Maybe, but like Willy is always saying, innocent until proven guilty."

"I like guilty until proven innocent better,"

Emma said. She placed a bowl in front of Jennifer. "Strawberries over oat bran, and a slice of wheat toast. You're not eating right, Jennifer, and I'm beginning to see it in your face. You have tired lines around your mouth, and dark circles under your eyes. I'm glad you have the next four days off. It will do you good."

Jennifer poured milk on her cereal, not at all convinced having all that time on her hands would do her any good, because she knew she wouldn't be able to relax. But for Emma's sake, she managed a smile, and said, "I'll try and forget about it, Emma, and get on with the weekend. Promise."

Emma nodded, but Jennifer could see the concern in her eyes.

Jennifer found Willy tossing bits of bread to the ducks, and noted he was wearing jeans and a casual shirt. She gave him a hug, and grinned. "I take it you have the day off too?"

"Nothing doing until Tuesday. Even the bad guys are being good. There's nothing like a big holiday to turn everybody into angels. Judge Stoker and Judge Jones are both on the barbecue committee, so I guess that's part of it. Can't work on something important like that if you're stuck in court. I don't know if you noticed, but even the sun is smiling.''

When they were kids, Willy always used to say the sun was smiling if it was warm, and frowning if it was cold. She lifted her face to its warmth, and nodded. ''I can feel fall in the air, and see the beginning of it everywhere, yet on days like this, I can truly believe we might have a few more days left of summer. The sun feels wonderful. I'm glad I wore a sundress.''

''So am I, and you look wonderful. I thought you'd be all gloomy and down. Unless, of course, you haven't read the morning paper.''

''I read it, and I'll admit it was a surprise. But maybe it's just as well. At this stage of the investigation, letting the town in on all the details would probably only hinder the investigation. If we can call it that. With nothing to work with—''

Willy shook his head. ''Forget about it for now, Jenny.''

''That's what Emma told me this morning. She said I should put the whole thing on hold for a few days, and enjoy the festivities, but I don't know if I can.''

Willy sat down beside her, and handed her a slice of bread. ''Sure you can, and you can begin by feeding the ducks. See that mallard over there?

The one preening his feathers? He'll take the bread right out of your hand.''

Jennifer broke off a piece of bread, held out her hand, and the mallard waddled up. After the bread was gone, and the duck had joined the others in the pond, Jennifer looked out over the expanse of trees and flowers. "It won't be long before the ducks head south for the long winter. Do you ever wonder where they go?''

"Someplace warm and cozy, I would imagine. Just like that little spot over there.''

He was pointing at the secluded spot where he'd spread out a blanket. When she saw the picnic basket, she said, "The deli would have been good enough, Willy. You didn't have to go to so much trouble.''

He gave her a lopsided grin. "I did go to the deli, Jenny. I just didn't want to carry it around in paper bags. Pastrami on rye, cheese, a basket of fruit, and bottled spring water. And while we're eating, I'm going to tell you about all the plans I have for us over the next few days. I figure if I keep you busy enough, you won't have time to think about Elmer Dodd.''

"What kind of plans?'' Jennifer asked, as they headed for the blanket.

"Well, for starters, there's a dance at the pavilion tonight, and then tomorrow morning, we'll attend the pancake breakfast right here in Calico Park. Then we'll walk to the town square and listen to the high school choir, and then Sunday, after church, we're going to the fair at the Grange.''

Willy lived with his widowed mother in the family home, and Jenny considered that now. ''And I suppose your mom is entering a pie and jam?''

''Yeah, she is. She said just this morning that this is the year she's going to beat out Emma, who always seems to take the blue ribbons.''

''And then?''

''And then . . . Well, they're holding a country-western dance at the Grange Sunday night. Thought that might be fun. We don't have to stay late. Monday is going to be a big day.''

Jennifer sighed. ''The parade in the morning, the barbecue on the green, and then the fireworks that night. ''I'm already exhausted, Willy.''

Willy handed her a pastrami sandwich, and chuckled. ''Good! By the way, can you do the 'Texas two-step'?''

''No, but I'll bet you're going to teach me.''

''Uh-huh. Along with the 'achy-breaky.' ''

Jennifer rolled her eyes, and bit into her sandwich.

They had the remnants of lunch packed away in the basket, and were lying on their stomachs, watching a group of kids play Frisbee on the other side of the pond, when Willy said, "Okay, out with it. You made an attempt to eat lunch and carry on a congenial conversation, but I can see that 'look' in your eyes. You're thinking about Elmer Dodd, and it's really bothering you."

Jennifer flushed. "Sorry."

"Don't be. He's on my mind too. Too many unanswered questions, Jenny."

"I know, and there doesn't seem to be much chance of getting the answers."

"If I didn't know better, I'd say he's committed the perfect crime, or somebody has."

"Yeah, but you know better, because nobody commits the perfect crime. There is something out there waiting for us, Willy. Some shred of a clue we're overlooking. I know it. I can *feel* it."

Willy sighed. "Usually you're the one who has all these feelings, but this time, I feel it too. Meanwhile, I think we should take Emma's advice, put this on hold for a few days and enjoy the festivities. Even a couple of super sleuths have to have some fun once in awhile."

He was grinning at her, and she stuck out her tongue. "Okay, super sleuth, have it your way.

But you'd better believe if I get a giant brainstorm, nothing is going to stop me from pursuing it.''

"Not even if you're winning the sack race?"

"Not even if I'm winning the egg toss, or the balloon race, the three-legged race, or the obstacle course, or . . .''

Willy leaned over and gave her a gentle kiss. It was nice, and stopped her in mid-sentence. When she looked at him, he was grinning down at her, with a twinkle in his eye. "Not even a kiss?"

"Well, maybe a kiss . . .''

"Uh-huh, and I'll remember that. Shall we put this stuff in my car, and then walk over to Fenten's for an ice-cream cone? I'll buy."

"Three scoops of marble fudge, and you're on," Jennifer said, with her heart full of love. Willy Ashton was a special guy, and she was very lucky to have him in her life.

Chapter Eight

The final day's activities were held on the greenbelt that ran along the river, and Emma had picked out a location on a shady rise that was close to the river, close to the barbecue pits, yet far enough away from the crowd to give them a little privacy. Jennifer was very pleased with Emma's choice because she was exhausted, and wanted to do nothing more than stretch out on a blanket and watch the puffy clouds drift by in the powder-blue sky. Willy had not only kept her busy over the weekend, he'd worn her out, proving his theory that if he kept her busy enough, she wouldn't think about Elmer Dodd. For the most part, it had worked, with the exception of yesterday at the Grange. Dodd had been one of the apple pie judges, and the blue ribbon had gone to a pretty dark-haired woman named Constance Brook who had moved to Calico from Lincoln three months earlier, after a nasty divorce. She lived in the mobile home park out on Route 5 between the new mall and Boodie's Roadhouse, and the rumors had started the minute she drove her chuggedy Ford into town and began batting her eyelashes at all the men. She said she was looking for a job, but nobody believed her. More than likely she was looking for a husband, and preferably one with money. As far as Jennifer was concerned, she'd proved it yesterday, when she began flirting with Dodd. She'd made a true spectacle of herself, hanging all over him and laughing dramatically in a high, tinkly voice. Even worse, the woman's apple pie tasted like cardboard, and Dodd, who hadn't been able to take his eyes off her from the moment she'd flounced onto the grounds, had undoubtedly swayed the judges. But he hadn't been a part of the jam judging, and Emma had promptly won a blue ribbon for her "Strawberry Delight," partly making up for the travesty.

The only other downside had been this morning, when Dodd had ridden by on a "Cornhusker" float during the parade, smiling and waving at the cheering crowd.

At the moment, he was down on the green with the mayor, mingling with the crowd, shaking hands, and no doubt counting votes. He definitely had more gall than ten men put together.

"It takes one to know one," Jennifer muttered, pouring lemonade into a tall plastic glass.

Emma snorted. "If you're talking about Elmer Dodd and Donald Attwater, I agree. I don't remember the mayor wearing that kind of getup before he started getting chummy with Dodd. Wonder if he knows how ridiculous he looks."

Both men were wearing white linen suits and Panama hats, and Jennifer grinned. "Short, squat, fat bellies and long cigars. They could be bookends."

Emma added, "Corrupt bookends. Just the thought of the mayor selling Elmer Dodd that plot of land, knowing full well it was worthless, sets my teeth on edge. And you know, thinking back through the years, I can't remember one blamed thing he's done for the town. A problem lands on his desk, and he tosses it back and says, 'Fix it.' Don't imagine Elmer Dodd would be any better. Providing, of course, he gets to the mayor's chair.

Oh boy, can't you just picture a murderer sitting in that chair, trying to run the town?''

"No, I can't, Emma, and it's a scary thought.''

Elmer Dodd and the mayor were moving from one group of picnickers to another, but when Dodd picked up a towheaded boy and gave him a hug, Jennifer had to look away. Worse, her grandfather was in the barbecue area, tending to the ribs with his cronies, and Willy was on the other side of the green, teaching his mother to play horseshoes. For some strange reason, being alone with Emma made Jennifer feel incredibly vulnerable, and she prayed with all her heart Elmer Dodd and the mayor wouldn't spot them up on the hill. Finally, when they moved off in another direction, she heaved a sigh of relief. But it was short-lived. The lesser of two evils, she reminded herself, as Cottie Anderson hobbled up the hill.

"Well, my my, I thought it was you,'' Cottie said, sitting down in a lawn chair and fanning her face with the bottom of the green cobbler's apron that partially covered her frilly white party dress. She also wore white gloves, dark nylons rolled down to the knees, and sneakers.

Cottie's eyes narrowed. "I don't understand why *you* didn't get hoodwinked into helping out, Emma. You look more fit than the rest of us.''

"Maybe it's because I learned to say 'no' a long time ago, Cottie, and it's good to see you, too."

"So what are you doing to help out, Miss Anderson?" Jennifer asked.

Cottie peered into the shadows. "Ah-hah, little Jennifer Gray. I didn't see you tucked in behind that big old tree. But I knew you had 'ta be around here somewhere. About the whole town is here, and what would a celebration be like if we didn't have little Jennifer Gray to brighten things up. My, my, don't you look pretty. Yellow shorts and blouse, the color of the sun. I used 'ta look good in yellow, but that was when my hair was dark. Think that was in sixty-eight. Or was it seventy-eight?"

She reached into a pocket and produced a roll of tickets. "Well, you asked what I'm doing 'ta help out. I'm selling raffle tickets, young lady. Twenty-five cents each, or five for a dollar. I've been all over trying 'ta drum up business. Can't believe how tight people are these days. Must be the war. Hard times on everybody."

Emma rolled her eyes. "What war, Cottie?"

"Why, the War of Hard Times, Emma. Where have *you* been?" She looked at the tickets in her hand. "Well, the prize is a twenty-five-dollar gift certificate 'ta the Mercantile, so you'd think everybody would take pity on an old soul like me with a bum knee and hip, stumbling around, trying 'ta do my job. Couldn't even get the mayor and Elmer Dodd 'ta buy one measly ticket.'' She lowered her voice. ''Doesn't what happened 'ta Elmer Dodd beat all? Why, when I read about it in the paper, I about had a case of the vapors. Skeleton bones found buried right on his property. The paper didn't say much, of course, but I just put it all together. I read the first story too, about the human bones and all, and I'll bet you anything it's poor Bernice and that traveling salesman. Wonder who shot 'em. Hmmmm. The sheriff ought 'ta be told. Now you understand, I don't like Elmer Dodd, and that's not the reason I'm saying this, but maybe *he* shot 'em. Maybe he found out Bernice was running off with the traveling salesman and shot 'em. Shot 'em dead. Deader than a doornail.''

''I'll take ten tickets,'' Jennifer said quickly, with her mind on overload, because suddenly she knew the elusive ''something'' she hadn't been able to put her finger on was Cottie Anderson, and it all stemmed from their conversation at the market.

Cottie beamed. ''Well, thank you, young lady. That's mighty generous of you.''

While they exchanged money and tickets, Jennifer said, "When we were talking in the market the other day, you mentioned the traveling salesman. You also said Bernice Dodd was your hairdresser. I know for a fact hairdressers confide in their customers, and vice versa. Did Bernice ever talk to you about the traveling salesman? And I wouldn't worry about confidentiality, Miss Anderson. It's been sixteen years."

Cottie Anderson's eyes narrowed in thought. "*Hmmmm.* Well, no, she never did talk about that man, now that I think about it, except to say he was a mighty handsome man. I heard a lot about him after she ran off with him, though. The whole town was a buzz. But then Elmer Dodd was making a big 'ta-do over it too, telling everybody about how Bernice had run off with the salesman, trying 'ta get sympathy."

Emma said, "As I recall, nobody actually saw him."

"No, don't suppose they did. At least I don't know of anybody who did. Or if they did, nobody remembered him."

"Did she ever talk to you about her relationship with her husband?" Jennifer asked, exchanging glances with Emma.

"Uh-huh. All the time." She looked over her

shoulder, and lowered her voice again. "Used 'ta tell me about their fights. 'Course I wasn't surprised. Elmer Dodd always had a nasty temper. But then, so did Bernice."

Jennifer took a deep breath. "I heard they had a fight in the Mercantile one day, and she threatened to kill him some night while he was in bed, and put an end to their miserable marriage. Or words to that effect."

"She told me that too, but I didn't take her seriously, even though she owned a gun and claimed she knew how 'ta use it."

Jennifer's breath accelerated. "Really. What kind of a gun?"

Cottie Anderson shrugged. "I don't know anything about guns, and she never said . . . Hmmmm, she did say it had a pretty little pearl handle. Course that was told to me confidentially, 'cause Elmer didn't know she had a gun. That was *her* secret. Then it was *my* secret, 'cause she told me. Guess that was back in forty-eight."

Emma sighed. "You were in high school in forty-eight, Cottie."

Cottie beamed. "I sure was. I went to school with Wes Gray. Guess you know he's pastor of the Calico Christian Church." She blinked. "Well, of course you know."

Jennifer's pulse had quickened at the mention of the pearl-handled gun, and she cleared her throat. "Would you like a glass of lemonade, Miss Anderson? You look a little flushed."

Cottie was fanning her face with the apron again, and nodded. "It's all this heat. Almost fall, and you'd never know it. Or maybe it's all this talk about that poor woman. Bernice was her name. Bernice Dodd. She was a nice lady. Used 'ta make little curls on top of my head. She knew all about fixing hair 'cause she liked to look pretty. Pretty for the salesman, and Joe Daily."

Jennifer poured Cottie a glass of lemonade, and waited until she had taken a sip before she said, "When we were talking in the market, you mentioned Joe Daily. Supposedly he worked at the dairy? You said Bernice was 'sweet on him.' Elmer Dodd claims his wife was sweet on the traveling salesman too, but he didn't take it seriously, because she liked to flirt."

Cottie scowled. "Now you understand, I liked Bernice. She used 'ta make pretty little curls on top of my head. Used 'ta get my hair just the right color too. Think I was blond, back in those days. Let's see. Guess I was about forty-something. My mother, God rest her soul, was beginning to feel poorly then. . . ." She blinked and frowned.

"What was I saying? Ah-huh. Bernice was a flirt. That she was. But that didn't mean she didn't love Elmer. Said he was the only man for her, but guess that was before he started showing his true colors, and she found out what kind of a man she married. Made her life miserable, he did. And then along came Joe Daily. Big, strapping, handsome man, who made her feel pretty, like she was a real lady. She used 'ta say she wished she'd met him first. She said he was soooo handsome, and a charmer. One time she said she might even run away with him, and that's why I was so surprised when she ran off with the salesman."

Jennifer could feel the excitement building inside of her. Even her hands were shaking, and she folded them in her lap. Was Elmer Dodd the killer? Or was it possible they had a love triangle on their hands involving Bernice, the traveling salesman, and Joe Daily? And was it possible one of those two men was the killer? "I think you said Joe Daily took off? Was that before or after Bernice disappeared?"

Cottie ran a gloved hand through her bright red hair. "About the same time, as I recollect. My neighbor on the right? That's old Barney Watkins. A widower, you know, and just the nicest man. He mows my lawn every week. Well, Barney played pool with Joe Daily out at Boodie's Road-house. Now, I never approved of that place, you understand, but Barney never did much in the way of recreation, and he used 'ta tell me all about it. And my oh my, how he liked 'ta play pool. Used 'ta win too. 'Course he doesn't play pool any-more. Has a bad back. Anyway, he told me all about Joe Daily, and how he was sorry for the man 'cause he didn't have any family. Came in one day from Council Bluffs looking for work, and got on at the dairy. Or maybe it was Omaha . . . Hmmmm. Barney hated 'ta see him spend all his money on pool, 'cause Elmer Dodd paid him so poorly. When Bernice first mentioned Joe Daily, I knew just who she was talking about. And that's how come I knew he was a mighty hand-some man. She said he was, and I believed her. Said the salesman was handsome too.''

''And you say Joe Daily left about the same time Bernice disappeared?''

''That he did. I remember going into town for a permanent, and the beauty shop was closed. That same day, I heard all the rumors about her running off with the salesman. That night, or maybe it was the next night, Barney went out 'ta Boodie's Roadhouse for his regular game of pool, but Joe wasn't there. Found out the next day he'd quit his

job, and was on his way south. I remember thinking 'ta myself he was probably upset when he
found out about Bernice and the salesman.''

Cottie struggled to her feet. "Well, as nice as
this has been, talking 'ta you, best I be on my
way. I still have lots of tickets 'ta sell. Thanks for
the lemonade now, and . . . Well, best I just say
this, Emma. You look marvelous. Years younger.
One of these days, you'll have 'ta tell me your
secret.''

"Take care," Emma said, but her eyes were on
Jennifer.

Jennifer waited until the woman was out of ear-
shot before she said, "I know you're going to
think I'm crazy, but . . .''

"I know exactly what you're thinking," Emma
interrupted. "The pearl-handled gun belonged to
Bernice, and Dodd used it to kill them.''

"That's right, and if we can prove Bernice
owned the gun . . .''

Emma took a deep breath. "You'd have one
more piece of the puzzle.''

"But there's more, Emma. What if Bernice was
involved with the traveling salesman, *and* Joe
Daily? What if it was a lovers' triangle?''

Emma sucked in her breath. "Then one of those

two men could be the killer, and that means he's long gone. And how are you going to prove that?''

''I don't know, but it's definitely a possibility. And even worse, as much as I dislike Elmer Dodd and everything he stands for, maybe he was telling the truth.''

Emma said, ''I saw the sheriff about a half-hour ago. He was heading toward the barbecue pit. Best you find him, and see what he has to say. I just feel this coming to an end in my bones! First one piece of the puzzle, and then another!''

Aware that they still had to prove Elmer Dodd pulled the trigger, no matter whose gun it was, or they had to prove he was innocent, by way of finding the real killer, Jennifer hurried down the trail.

She found her grandfather slathering barbecue sauce over a rack of ribs, and her heart warmed at the sight of his happy face. He was wearing a white chef's apron covered with sauce, and was waving the basting brush around for emphasis, as he tried to get a point across to Cracker Martin. She gave both men a hug, while something else tugged at her thoughts. Something to do with Cracker . . .

''Ah-ha, Jennifer. Just the little lady I want to see. I was just telling Cracker here that it's time he started coming to church again. He says it would bring back too many memories of the time when his wife was alive, and when Elvis was a pup. I say those are the kinds of memories he should cherish, and draw strength from.''

Cracker was looking wonderful these days, and was becoming a part of the community again, but Jennifer had the feeling church wasn't on his agenda. She also had the feeling his wife had been the one responsible for getting him there in the first place, so her grandfather was fighting a losing battle. But now wasn't the time to get into it, and so she simply said, ''If anybody can talk Cracker into attending church, you can, Grandfather. Have you seen the sheriff?''

Wes's eyes narrowed over his granddaughter. ''Oh-oh. You see that look, Cracker? Something's afoot. I saw the sheriff about ten minutes ago, sweetheart. He was talking to Willy over by the wading pool.''

Cracker gave Jennifer a toothy grin, and then looked at Wes. ''I'd say she's playing detective again, Pastor Wes. Female detective. Just like my Addy used to say, 'Someday, the world is going to be run by women, Cracker. Mark my words.' Can see this little lady president of the Uooonited States. She does what she sets her mind to, and don't care much about how hard she has to work at it, either. Or what anybody thinks. That's what makes a good politician. Fight for what's right no matter what anybody says. She'd make a good head doctor too. She sure brought me out of the dumps when old Elvis died. And now she's pushing me into joining up at the senior citizens' center.''

Jennifer kissed Cracker's cheek. ''Well, you're thinking about it, so I don't want to hear any complaints.''

''Yeah, and she's even got me talking to the sheriff again, and that's really something. Still think he's a weenie, and still won't vote for him if and when he runs for sheriff again, but guess a handshake is better than a feud.''

Jennifer quickly assembled all the questions she wanted to ask, because the time was now. ''I know you were a crack shot in your day, and that's where you got the nickname 'Cracker.' I also know you won a lot of medals at the gun club. Did Elmer Dodd's father ever belong to the gun club? Just wondered, because Elmer Dodd has his father's gun collection. . . .''

''Yeah, his daddy belonged to the gun club. Used to say he wanted Elmer to join, but he never did.''

"Do you suppose that was because Elmer was afraid of guns?"

Cracker nodded. Elmer's daddy didn't take too kindly to that. Didn't want his son to be a sissy."

"What about Elmer's wife?"

Cracker's shaggy brows drew together. "You mean, did she belong to the gun club?"

"I was just wondering."

"Not that I recall, but I wasn't around much in those days. My Addy's health was failing then. . . ." He swallowed deeply. "Those days are long gone, but seem like yesterday. Anyway, about the only woman I know of who belonged to the gun club was Martha Anderson."

Jennifer frowned. "Martha Anderson?"

"Cottie Anderson's mother," Wes said. "That was long before she took sick, of course, and I'll admit a few of us around town didn't like the idea of that woman owning a gun. She always seemed to be feuding with Elmer Dodd's father. Even in church, and one time she threatened the butcher with the gun."

Cracker nodded. "I remember some fights at the range that put a lot of gray in my hair."

Wes sighed. "Martha never did have all her faculties."

Cracker nodded. "And the daughter wasn't

much better. Martha used to bring Cottie out to the range all the time, and Cottie took to shooting like a duck takes to water. I always thought they both had a screw loose, and I guess that hasn't changed. Saw Cottie earlier today, and she still looks and acts crazy. She called me Barney, whoever the devil that is, and wanted to know if I was still playing pool.''

"Barney is her next-door neighbor," Jennifer said. "I was talking to her a few minutes ago, and she mentioned him. She said he mows her lawn every week. . . .''

"No way," Wes said. "Barney Watkins died at least fifteen years ago. He was a widower, and I used to see him on the street, head down, looking so sad, it about broke my heart. Then one day I heard he'd died in his sleep.''

"Just proves Cottie is loony," Cracker said. "And those little white gloves. She used to wear 'em when she was shooting with her mother, and she's still wearing 'em.''

Jennifer suddenly felt lightheaded. It wasn't possible, but what if? She gave Cracker a shaky smile, and tried to keep her voice light. "Do you remember what kind of a gun Martha Anderson owned?''

Her grandfather was busily brushing more

sauce on the ribs, but she could see the expression on his face. And it was much more than curious interest.

"Hmmmm," Cracker said. "As I recollect, it was a twenty-two. Little pearl handle. Cottie used it to shoot too, and both women were crack shots. I remember Elmer's daddy having a fit, and getting all over Elmer's case, because he was afraid of guns. He'd say, 'Look at Cottie Anderson, and take a lesson!' "

Wes kept his back turned while he tended to the ribs, but Jennifer knew what he was thinking. She desperately wanted to tell him about the conversation with Cottie Anderson, and that his thoughts were in tune with her own, but didn't want to do it in front of Cracker.

"How much longer are you going to be here?" she asked him finally.

Although Wes turned around with a smile on his face, Jennifer could see the astonishment in his eyes. Was he also saying to himself, 'It's not possible, but what if?' He swallowed. "Not long. I'm ready for a break."

"Okay, then I'll meet you back at our picnic site in a little while."

She gave both men another hug, and hurried off to find the sheriff and Willy, trying to restrain her emotions that were bubbling up. Innocent until proven guilty, she kept telling herself, but what if . . .

"Dr. Gray?"

Jennifer turned around. It was Dan Wise, and his smile was wide and sincere. She shook the man's hand, and returned his smile.

"Just wanted you to know Einstein is doing fine. I thought about bringing him today, but decided to leave him home. Moved out of the cottage, by the way, and quit my job at the dairy. I'm working out at the mall now, cashiering in the bookstore. Found a little house on the east side of town. Not much more than I was paying for the cottage, and Einstein has a fenced-in backyard, so I can keep him out of trouble. Anyway, now that I'm making more money, I'll be able to pay the vet bill."

"There is no hurry, Mr. Wise, and I'm truly glad to hear you've gotten away from the dairy, and that Einstein is doing so well. We'd like to see him in a couple of weeks, but then I suppose Dr. Copeland has already set up the appointment?"

"He did. I was hoping to see him today. I'd like to thank him too."

"He's here somewhere with his wife. But if you don't see him, I'll tell him."

Dan Wise lowered his eyes and bit at his lip. "I have to ask, Dr. Gray. I read about the human bones found on that plot of land south of town, and kind of put it together. I mean, I read the first story, about the kids finding a bone when they were playing, and now I'm wondering if . . . well, did Einstein find a . . . well . . ."

"Yes, he did," Jennifer said. "It was one of the phalanges in a finger. We knew about it that day we talked to you at the clinic, but of course we couldn't say anything."

"Then that's why you asked me all those questions about where Einstein might have gone when he was out roaming?"

"That's right. We had the feeling the finger had been attached to a skeleton, but we also knew pinpointing the location would be next to impossible."

He shook his head. "And then those two boys found a bone. . . ."

"Uh-huh, and everything sort of escalated from there."

"They didn't say in the paper, but I was just wondering who it was, and . . . Well, you know. Was that poor person murdered, or . . ."

Like a bolt out of the blue, the final piece of the puzzle slipped into place. Jennifer found herself trying to suck in air. "I-I don't know...."

Dan Wise frowned. "Are you okay? You look kinda shaky."

"It's been a taxing day," she said quickly. "But thanks for your concern. Enjoy the picnic, and give Einstein a hug."

A few minutes later, Jennifer found Willy and the sheriff watching a volleyball game, and pulled them aside. "We have to talk," she said, trying to keep her voice under control. "But not here. Where is your mom, Willy?"

"She's with a group of friends on the other side of the park...."

"You look pretty darned strange, Jennifer," the sheriff said. "Has something happened?"

"You have no idea. Grandfather is going to meet us at our picnic spot in a few minutes, so let's hurry!"

The men didn't have to be coaxed, and trotted to keep up with Jennifer as she led the way.

Chapter Nine

When they reached the little hill where Emma and her grandfather were waiting, Jennifer tried to catch her breath and said, "Did you tell Emma, Grandfather?"

"Wes shook his head. "No, because I thought you could do a better job than me, though to tell you the truth, I still don't know what we've got. I have a sneaking hunch, of course, but I've been telling myself it can't be. Boy, oh boy, I just knew this day was going to end on a bad note. Just had a feeling. Tell me if I'm wrong, sweetheart, but I think Cracker Martin just opened up a whole can of worms."

Jennifer waited until the sheriff and Willy had pulled up chairs, before she said, "You're not wrong. First of all, has anybody seen Cottie Anderson?''

Emma pointed down the hill. ''She's near the tennis court, talking to Elmer Dodd and the mayor. I would suspect she's still trying to talk them into buying some raffle tickets.''

Jennifer caught a glimpse of Cottie's flaming red hair, and shuddered. ''I don't want everybody to scream at once, but I think Cottie Anderson is the killer.''

Jennifer didn't get screams, just wide eyes and gasps.

Wes was the first to speak. ''I knew you were onto something when you started asking Cracker all those questions.''

''I tried to be nonchalant about it, but I'm not so sure I succeeded. I couldn't believe the thoughts going through my head.''

''She's always been as crazy as a bedbug,'' Emma muttered.

''That doesn't prove she's the killer,'' Jennifer reasoned. ''But cold, hard facts might.''

Willy took Jennifer's hand, and gave it a squeeze. ''Why don't you just start at the beginning, Jenny.''

''Okay. First of all, Emma and I had a little conversation with Cottie earlier, and she made a comment that slipped right over us, because we were so intent on something else she said.''

Emma nodded. ''Like how Bernice owned a little pearl-handled gun that Elmer didn't know anything about, and that made us wonder if Elmer found the gun, and used it to kill Bernice and the traveling salesman.''

Jennifer went on. ''And then she told us that Bernice was a flirt, and that she was also interested in Joe Daily, a man who worked at the dairy, and left town about the same time Bernice supposedly ran off with the salesman. At that point, we wondered if Elmer was actually telling the truth, and that maybe what we really had was a lovers' triangle. Of course, the only way to know who pulled the trigger would be to identify the other body. Maybe it's the salesman, or maybe it's Joe Daily.'' Jennifer looked at the sheriff and Willy, and said, ''Is any of this making any sense?''

''I'm following you so far,'' the sheriff said.

''But now you don't think that's the way it happened?'' Willy asked.

''No, I don't, because Cracker Martin just told me that Martha Anderson, Cottie's mother, owned a pearl-handled gun, and both women used it to target practice at the range, and both were crack shots. He also told me that Elmer was afraid of guns, much to his father's dismay. He also said Cottie always wore little white gloves when she was shooting, just like she's wearing now. You said you thought either the gun had been in the ground too long, or that the killer wiped the prints off the gun, Sheriff Cody, but what if the killer wore gloves?''

The sheriff shook his head. ''This is really reaching, Jennifer. What would be the motive?''

''Jealousy. What if Cottie had a crush on Joe Daily? She went on and on about how handsome he was. She also said he was a charmer, and he made Bernice feel pretty, like a real lady. But what if she was really talking about herself?''

''I think we should go back to that time to understand this. You knew Cottie's mother, Sheriff. What was the relationship like between mother and daughter?''

''Cottie was under her mother's thumb all her life,'' the sheriff said. ''She never dated, and then after her mother took sick, Cottie became the primary caregiver.''

''Father?''

''He walked out on them when Cottie was a kid. Walked right out of Calico, too.''

Jennifer nodded. ''Okay, so what if Cottie met

Joe Daily, and he began to charm her? Remember, she was in her forties at the time. And if she was starving for attention, it all makes sense. Let's say Joe Daily led her on, for whatever reason, and to make sure her mother didn't find out about it, they always met somewhere where they would have privacy.''

Emma clucked her tongue. ''Like on Elmer Dodd's property. Out in the middle of nowhere, and that's why she buried the bodies there. What better place?''

''That's what I think,'' Jennifer said. ''I also think Bernice was involved with both men, but Elmer didn't know about Joe Daily. That's why he thought she ran off with the salesman. For all we know, the salesman took off, and that's why his car was never found. But then that left a different kind of triangle. Two women and a man.''

Willy shook his head. ''Then you think the other body, or skeleton, is Joe Daily?''

''I do. I think Cottie shot them and buried them, along with the gun. If Emma's right, and they used to meet on that plot of land, she probably knew it well, and knew where to bury the bodies so she wouldn't have to dig through hardpan. And we can't overlook her stature. She's a large woman, and sixteen years ago, she probably had more than enough strength to do all that digging.''

Willy said, ''But she didn't know about the underground stream.''

''No, she didn't, and I think that all that stuff she told us about Bernice's little pearl-handled gun was to throw us off the track. I mean, we can't very well question Bernice, can we? She reads the newspaper, so she knows what's been going on, and when she read about the sheriff finding human bones, she knew she had to do something. What better way than to drop the hint that Bernice owned a pearl-handled gun, and put the suspicion on Elmer Dodd? Everybody thinks she's crazy, and maybe she is, but there is a part of her mind that works like a steel trap. I also think she made it a point to talk to us today, so she could give us all those little tidbits. I think she set us up.''

The sheriff ran a hand through his hair. ''It makes sense, but it's still speculation, Jennifer. Thinking it is one thing, but proving it is quite another.''

Jennifer gave him a sly smile. ''What if I told you she really slipped up?''

''I'd listen.''

''Remember I said Cottie said something that

went right over our heads?'' She pointed at the sheriff and Willy. ''While I was looking for you guys, I ran into Dan Wise, who owns the dog that nearly choked to death on a bone.''

Willy said, ''The bone that started the whole incredible chain of events.''

''That's right. Well, he said he read about everything in the paper, and wanted to know if the poor person had been murdered, or words to that effect. And that's when it hit me. Cottie said she read about it in the paper too. . . .''

Emma groaned. ''Lordy, how could we let *that* slip by? She said she'd bet anything that it was Bernice and the traveling salesman, and she wondered who shot them. How did she know they'd been shot? It wasn't in the paper. All John, Jr., mentioned was the fact that human bones had been found, period.''

Silence followed. Finally, the sheriff said, ''I don't see a way out of it. I have to take her in for questioning.''

Willy poured a glass of lemonade, and took a long drink before he said, ''You think she'll confess? Seems to me you'll have the same problem with her as you had with Dodd. You still have to prove she pulled the trigger.''

Wes sighed. ''And even if she confesses, what

will you have? A poor demented woman who, at any given moment, probably couldn't tell us what day it is.''

"I know," Jennifer said, "and it's so sad. She told us all about her next-door neighbor, and we assumed he was alive, yet you said he's been dead for fifteen years, Grandfather.''

"*Hr-rump*," Emma muttered. "That part of it might be sad, but I haven't got much sympathy for somebody who could shoot two people in cold blood. She belongs in the loony bucket.''

"That's the loony bin," Wes said dismally. "Such a waste.''

Willy nodded. "That's probably where she'd end up. Even if she confesses, it probably wouldn't go to trial. More than likely she'd be found insane, and placed in a mental institution.''

Emma looked down the hill, where Cottie was hobbling along the path, and sighed. "Yeah, I guess it's pretty sad after all. I remember what she looked like back then. Kinda pretty, in a big, buxom way. Though I never could keep track of the color of her hair. . . .'' Tears shimmered in Emma's eyes. "I was just thinking that maybe Jennifer should talk to her before you haul her in, Sheriff. I don't think she would fight you, but you never know. We all know how a pig squeals when it gets cornered, and the park is full of families.''

Jennifer sucked in her breath. ''Oh, God, Emma . . .''

''God will be right there over your shoulder, sweetheart,'' Wes said gently. ''And I think it's a good idea. I have the feeling she doesn't trust men, and maybe you could soften it a little for her.''

''But why me?'' Jennifer asked.

''Well, I sure can't do it,'' Emma said. ''We've always been at odds. Besides, she likes you. I can tell.''

Jennifer looked at the sheriff, and he nodded. ''I think it's a good idea too, Jennifer, but don't tell her we suspect her. Just tell her I want to talk to her in my office. Make it sound like I need her help. I'd like her to go with me peacefully, without causing a ruckus, because I sure don't want to ruin everybody's day. And don't worry. I won't be far.''

''That goes for me too, Jenny,'' Willy said. ''I'll be by your side in seconds, if there's a sign of trouble.''

Jennifer braced herself, and headed down the hill, muttering, ''I think I'm outnumbered.''

Trying to remind herself she was dealing with

a sick woman instead of a cold-blooded killer, yet looking over her shoulder just the same, to make sure the sheriff and Willy were within calling distance, Jennifer made her way along the path, dreading what was ahead of her more than anything she could remember. She finally caught up with Cottie near the rose garden.

Cottie saw her and beamed. "My, my, it's little Jennifer Gray. I thought I recognized all that blond hair. My hair used 'ta be that color."

Jennifer's heart twisted. No matter what, Cottie Anderson was a human being, a soul who had lived in torment all her life. "Your hair is very pretty now, Miss Anderson. Let's sit down and talk. I don't know about you, but this day has completely worn me out."

"Me too," Cottie said. "Course, I'm getting on in years, and I've got a bad hip and knee. I guess I should go over 'ta the new hospital across the river . . ."

"We can sit here," Jennifer broke in, motioning toward a bench. "It's in the shade, and should be a little cooler."

Cottie sat down, and fanned her face with her green cobbler's apron. "Never minded the sun when I was younger."

"Did you sell all your raffle tickets?" Jennifer asked.

"I did. Sold the last one 'ta a young man." She patted the apron. "Lots of money. Joe would be proud."

Jennifer's breath caught in her throat. "Joe?"

She shook her head. "I meant Barney. He wanted 'ta come today, but his back's been bothering him. He's the nicest man. Mows my lawn all the time."

"You mentioned Joe. Joe Daily?"

Her eyes looked vacant for a moment, and then a smile cracked her wrinkled face. "Joe. He was so handsome. Made you feel like a real lady."

"Made you feel like a real lady?" Jennifer asked, aware that the woman was exhausted from the activities of the day, which might be the reason for some of her confusion, but that she was also walking a very thin line between the past and the present.

"Joe Daily . . ." Cottie blinked, then frowned. "Did I say Joe? I meant Barney."

"Do you miss Barney?"

"Miss him? I guess. He would've been a big help today. He wanted 'ta come, but his back was bothering him."

"What about your mother?"

Cottie's frown deepened. "My mother didn't like picnics and town get-togethers."

"Did she like Barney?"

"She didn't know Barney. I made sure of that. We always met after it got dark, after my mother was asleep."

Jennifer took a deep, ragged breath. Not only was Cottie walking a fine line between the past and the present, she was mixing up Joe Daily and Barney Watkins.

While Jennifer was trying to decide if she should tell Cottie the sheriff wanted to talk to her, or wait a few minutes longer, Cottie muttered, "He told me I was beautiful. He told me he loved me, and that he was going 'ta take me away."

"Who told you you were beautiful, Miss Anderson?" Jennifer asked.

The woman's eyes misted over. "Joe Daily. He told me he was going 'ta take me away, and he would've too, but then *she* came along and spoiled everything."

"You mean Bernice?"

"I thought she was my friend. She used 'ta fix little curls on top of my head. But then Joe came along." Tears rolled down her cheeks. "I didn't mean 'ta do it. . . ."

Feeling something close to a panic attack, Jennifer looked around. The sheriff was standing under a tree, not more than ten feet away. And Willy wasn't more than a few feet behind them.

"Do you know the sheriff?" Jennifer asked, terrified the woman might bolt if she saw them. And what if Cottie confessed everything to her, but refused to talk to the sheriff? Would the confession hold up in court? It didn't matter, she reminded herself, because Willy said it wouldn't go that far. . . .

Cottie smiled through her tears. "Jim Cody? I know him. Nice man. I feel sorry for him, what with the town getting so big. Too many people now. Trouble all the time."

"He's standing right over there under a tree, Miss Anderson. I think he'd like to join us."

Cottie looked up, saw him, and waved.

"And my friend is here too. His name is Willy Ashton, and he's a very nice man."

"Not all men are nice, but the sheriff is nice," Cottie said. "Sheriff Jim Cody. Nice man. Used 'ta call him Buffalo Bill."

Willy moved up to the end of the bench, and Jennifer waited until the sheriff was standing in front of them, and the two had exchanged greetings, before she said, "Miss Anderson was just telling me about Joe Daily, Sheriff. Did you know him?''

''I didn't have the pleasure of knowing Joe Daily,'' the sheriff said warily.

The sheriff's eyes were on the big pockets in the cobbler's apron. Was he wondering if she had another gun?

''He was a nice man too,'' Cottie said. ''Handsome. Made me feel like a lady.''

''And didn't you say he made Bernice feel like a lady too?'' Jennifer asked.

Cottie waved an arm. ''Bernice wasn't a lady. She wasn't a friend.'' Tears filled her eyes again. ''I didn't want 'ta kill him. . . . He told me he was leaving town with Bernice.'' She gripped her hands into fists. ''Bernice, who always used 'ta make those pretty little curls on top of my head. I thought she was my friend. She had Elmer, and she had that salesman. Why did she have 'ta take Joe?'' She fanned her face with the apron, and rocked back and forth.

Satisfied Cottie didn't have a gun, Sheriff Cody sat down beside her, and took her hand. ''Did you kill Bernice too, Cottie?''

Cottie nodded. ''I had my mother's gun. Pretty little gun with a pearl handle. They had Joe's car all packed up and were leaving town. I knew it, 'cause Joe told me. He said he was in love with Bernice, and they were going away. Elmer was out of town, visiting Ronald, or is it Roland? Roland. Roland Dodd. He owns a meatpacking plant in Omaha, and has a tall son named Collin.'' She smiled at Jennifer. ''He's a veterinarian too. I remember his name 'cause I remember Collin Bender. He used 'ta sit in front of me in school. Think that was in sixty-four.''

''You said you were waiting for Bernice and Joe Daily?'' the sheriff asked.

''I was waiting for them outside that big old house across the river. I made them get in Joe's car, and made Joe drive out 'ta that plot of land where we used 'ta meet. And I shot them. I had a shovel, and I buried them, and I buried the gun. Didn't want 'ta shoot Joe. But I did, and then I drove Joe's car home and put it in my garage.''

Jennifer felt the blood drain from her face. ''Is . . . is the car still in your garage?''

''Still in the garage,'' Cottie muttered, ''full of their things. We have a little carport next 'ta the garage, and that's where I always park my mother's car. . . . She's been ailing lately, and doesn't care where I park the car. Of course, I don't get around as much as I used 'ta. . . . Didn't mean to kill Joe, but he didn't love me. Only said he did.

Barney said he loved me too, but then he had 'ta get nasty."

"Barney, your neighbor?" Jennifer asked.

"Barney, my neighbor on my right. Or maybe it's on the left. He saw the car in the garage. Guess that was back in fifty-five. Afternoon. It was raining. Barney has a bad back, but he didn't then. Used 'ta mow my lawn all the time. Had a bad back and took lots of naps. He said he loved me, and was coming 'ta dinner. I didn't want 'ta kill him, but he said he was going 'ta tell the sheriff about the car. . . ."

The sheriff cleared his throat. "You killed Barney Watkins?"

"Put a pillow over his face 'ta stop him from talking. He was asleep. He had a bad back, you know. He struggled, but I just kept pushing."

Muscles worked along the sheriff's jawline. "I remember the day Nettie got the call. I sent a deputy out to take care of it, and then J. C. Fowler picked up the body. Supposedly, he died in his sleep."

Cottie grunted. "J. C. Fowler. He calls himself a mortician, and the coroner, but he's a fake. He made my mother up 'ta look ten years younger after she died. Even put rouge on her cheeks, and my mother wouldn't allow a stick of makeup in the house. Had 'ta have the coffin closed for the services,'cause I didn't want anybody to see her. Guess that was back in fifty-two. Joe didn't have a service. . . . I buried him. . . .''

Cottie was weeping openly now, and looked at least a hundred years old.

''I'd like to take you to my office,'' the sheriff said softly. ''That way, we can have a nice long talk.''

Cottie nodded. ''I have 'ta call Barney. . . .''

''We'll call Barney from my office,'' the sheriff said. ''Do you have an attorney?''

She mumbled, ''Gobel Norris. Nice man too. Haven't seen him in ages, but then I don't get around much anymore, what with my bad hip and knee. One of these days, I have to go 'ta that new hospital across the river. . . .''

The sheriff offered Cottie his arm. ''Well, then, we'll take it nice and slow.''

Aware that she had tears on her own cheeks, Jennifer watched them until they rounded a curve in the path, and then closed her eyes.

Willy sat down beside her, and put an arm around her shoulder. ''Just about the time you think you've seen everything, something like this comes along,'' he said with a sigh.

Jennifer wiped at her eyes and blew her nose.

"I don't know what I feel, Willy. I know Cottie is mentally ill, but I keep thinking about those poor people. And Barney Watkins. Dear God, what a shock! And to think she's had Joe Daily's car in her garage all these years."

"It's a damned shame," Willy said. "She's had to live with her guilt all these years too. I'm sure it added to her mental problems. I also have the feeling she would've taken the truth to her grave if that sinkhole hadn't opened up."

Jennifer couldn't answer him right away, but when she did, her words were heartfelt. "I learned something today, Willy. The truth, no matter how important, can also be bittersweet. We owe Elmer Dodd an apology. I can just imagine how he's going to feel when he finds out the salesman wasn't the only other man in Bernice's life."

Willy gave her a hug. "I don't think we owe him an apology, Jenny. We had every reason to suspect him. His type breeds suspicion, but . . ."

"I know, you don't have to say it. Innocent until proven guilty. I think I finally understand what that really means. It also makes me realize what the sheriff has to go through, day in and day out. He was sworn to uphold the law, no matter what, but it can't be easy."

"Especially when he's faced with something

like this. Let's go back to the picnic, Jenny. Wes and Emma are waiting, and probably worried sick.''

Jennifer nodded, and took his hand. There were no answers, of course. No answers that made any sense. Cottie Anderson had lived with her grief and guilt for sixteen long years, and Jennifer could only hope that now she could finally find peace.

Huddled in blankets because of the chill in the night air, Jennifer sat between her grandfather and Emma on the little rise overlooking the river. Willy sat behind her, with a hand on her shoulder, and she could feel the tenderness of his touch, as the skyrockets and bombs burst overhead. Brilliant white dahlias exploded against the velvet black sky, followed by red, blue, green and golden fountains of shimmering lights. The fireworks display was dazzling, and continued on for almost twenty minutes, reflecting across the shimmering water, as the town of Calico watched with upturned faces.

The sheriff hadn't come back to the park, but he had sent word by way of Manny Pressman. After calling in her attorney and talking to Cottie at length, he had taken her to the new hospital across the river, where she would be cared for until the court could hear her case. Willy was certain she would be found mentally incompetent, and the rest would only be a matter of formality. More important, she would get the help she needed. Elmer Dodd hadn't been told what happened yet, but the sheriff planned to talk to him in the morning, as well as give a press release to the newspaper. And then the whole town would know.

But life in Calico would go on. Jennifer couldn't think beyond that; she didn't want to. It was enough to feel the warmth and love of her family around her, and Willy's hand on her shoulder, while she watched the magical display above them. It was enough to realize how precious life really was.

Finally, it was over, and the day had come to an end.

"Are you okay, sweetheart?" Wes asked, as they were folding up the blankets.

She looked up at his handsome, caring face, and nodded. "I'm fine, Grandfather. Let's go home."

Home, where everything was right and wonderful, and maybe she could forget . . .

It was near daybreak when Jennifer made her way through the house, dragging a blanket behind her. She hadn't been able to sleep, and now she wanted to watch the sunrise, and the angels paint the sky. But what she found were thunderheads, a chilly breeze, and the threat of another storm. She curled up in a chair on the porch, and wrapped the blanket around her.

A few minutes later, Wes padded out, and handed her a cup of coffee.

"I didn't hear you in the kitchen," she said wearily. "I didn't even smell the coffee."

Wes pulled up a chair, and took her free hand. "Let it go, sweetheart. I know you've been up half the night, trying to sort it out, but sometimes, it's not our place to reason why. If you think you might find solace in church . . ."

"I keep thinking about Cottie, Grandfather, wondering how she could take a life so easily. Three lives . . . I know she's ill, and I'm trying to feel compassion, but I'm also filled with anger."

Wes kissed her fingers. "Look up at the sky, and tell me what you see."

"I see clouds. Dark, swirling clouds, and I can smell rain."

"And what does that make you think of?"

"A cozy fire in the fireplace, hot chocolate, and a Strauss waltz on the stereo. . . ." She took a deep breath. "And Mama, who loved stormy weather. Oh, Grandfather, I miss them both so much! Even after all these years, it seems like yesterday. I can even smell the sweet scent of Mama's hair, and Dad's shaving lotion. . . . They were taken from us in the cruelest possible way, and maybe that's why I feel so angry. Cottie took three lives, and she had no right to do that! Nobody has the right to take away what God created, except God. It makes a mockery of everything life stands for!''

"But it also reminds us of how inestimable life really is, Jennifer, and we should draw strength from that. Look up at the sky, and tell me what you see now."

Jennifer looked up. "I see a break in the clouds. I see the dawn . . . pale blue sky."

"And beyond? Farther than the eye can see?"

Jennifer raised her face as the breeze lifted and separated her hair into silky strands, and touched her skin like loving fingers. "It's okay to be confused, flustered, angry, and even afraid, as long as we can still feel compassion. I know it isn't always easy, but if you can draw strength from God's infinite wisdom, it will surely help."

She squeezed his hand. "You're my strength too, Grandfather. Thank you for being here."

"I'll always be here for you, sweetheart, as

long as God grants me life. And even later, in spirit. Just like your mama and daddy, who are never far away.'' He gave her a fetching wink. ''What would you say to having a brownie for breakfast? Emma hid them in the freezer, but we can use the microwave. Six left out of a dozen. Don't think that's too bad, do you?''

Jennifer smiled, and felt the warmth of it, and her grandfather's love, all the way to her heart. ''A brownie sounds wonderful,'' she said, taking his hand as they walked into the house.